"Andros," Polly whispered against his chest in her sleep.

Alexandros went rigid at the name he hadn't heard in years, not even during lovemaking. Then without even considering it, he was turning and facing her, gently shaking her shoulder. "Why don't you call me Andros anymore?"

"Andros was the man I fell in love with," she said in a voice that sounded more asleep than awake.

"And who is Alexandros?"

"The man I married." She made a snuffling sound and turned in her sleep. Away from him.

Alexandros wrapped his body around his wife, his entire perception of his life going through a painful metamorphosis.

USA TODAY bestselling author **Lucy Monroe** lives and writes in the gorgeous Pacific Northwest. While she loves her home, she delights in experiencing different cultures and places in her travels, which she happily shares with her readers through her books. A lifelong devotee of the romance genre, Lucy can't imagine a more fulfilling career than writing the stories in her head for her readers to enjoy.

Books by Lucy Monroe

Harlequin Presents

Million Dollar Christmas Proposal
Kosta's Convenient Bride
The Spaniard's Pleasurable Vengeance

By His Royal Decree

One Night Heir
Prince of Secrets

Ruthless Russians

An Heiress for His Empire
A Virgin for His Prize

Visit the Author Profile page
at Harlequin.com for more titles.

Lucy Monroe

AFTER THE
BILLIONAIRE'S
WEDDING VOWS...

HARLEQUIN
PRESENTS

Recycling programs for this product may not exist in your area.

ISBN-13: 978-1-335-40386-5

After the Billionaire's Wedding Vows…

Copyright © 2021 by Lucy Monroe

This edition published by arrangement with Harlequin Books S.A.

For questions and comments about the quality of this book, please contact us at CustomerService@Harlequin.com.

Harlequin Enterprises ULC
22 Adelaide St. West, 40th Floor
Toronto, Ontario M5H 4E3, Canada
www.Harlequin.com

Printed in U.S.A.

AFTER THE
BILLIONAIRE'S
WEDDING VOWS...

For the love of my life, because you have made more than thirty years together feel like it will never be long enough, because when we hit bumps, you launched your own bid and it was so worth working our way back to bliss. I love you so very much and I always, always will!

CHAPTER ONE

GREEK BILLIONAIRE AND societal icon Alexandros Kristalakis stepped into the hall, having wrapped up an in-
ternational call with one of his business interests in
America, unsurprised to find his wife waiting.

Unlike early in their marriage, Pollyanna was always punctual now.

Never late anymore, but neither was she spontane-
ous. Exuberant expressions of affection had disappeared
along with her spontaneity. He'd believed, at first, that
was the result of being pregnant the first time around, a
difficult period for her emotionally and physically. But
giving birth and early motherhood had not seen a rever-
sion to the old habits he'd enjoyed so much.

He could not complain. Pollyanna had worked too
hard to adjust to her new lifestyle as the wife of a billionaire Greek from an old and established family.

Coming from a far more relaxed background and
a family that had none of the societal expectations of
his own and the very different American culture, she'd
naturally found it a challenge. But not a challenge his
amazing and resilient wife could not meet.

Despite speaking almost no Greek to begin with, she
had attended the necessary social functions and lent

her newfound position to the support of worthy causes. With her naturally open nature and warm personality, she'd won over his friends and acquaintances, making a place for herself in Athens society not reliant wholly on her role as his wife.

Six months pregnant with their second child, the leggy brunette was more beautiful than the day they married.

Even if nowadays her warm personality was muted by a dignity more fitting to the name Anna his mother insisted she be called, rather than the more common Polly she used go by.

Her designer gown in the ice blue that had become known as her signature color clung to breasts that had grown at least a cup size since conception and fell in an elegant drape over her baby bump. His child growing inside his wife.

It gave him a sense of pride not even his most ruthlessly executed business deal ever had.

He gave her an openly appreciative look. "You look beautiful, *yineka mou*."

"That's what you pay the exorbitant fees to the stylists for." She didn't smile, or meet his eyes with her crystalline blue gaze.

She hardly ever did anymore. With him.

Other people still got the benefit of her warm nature, but he got the elegant wife who never spoke out of turn or reacted without thought. Except in the bedroom. There, she was still the passionate being he had known he could not live without.

He'd known she was something special the first time they went to bed together.

So he had asked her to marry him, instead of one of

the many proper Greek heiresses his mother had been throwing at him since uni days.

And she had said yes. Of course she had. Why wouldn't she?

He had been able to give Pollyanna a lifestyle she couldn't even have dreamed of.

Nevertheless it wasn't the expensive designer gown or glittering diamonds she'd opted to wear for the weekly family dinner, or even the silky chestnut hair swept up in an elegant twist, but the way she glowed with her pregnancy that had prompted his compliment.

Even looking a little tired, as she did now, she still took his breath away. "It is all you," he assured her.

She gave him a barely there tilt of her lips, clearly unimpressed by his praise.

She used to smile when he told her how beautiful she was to him, her expression open and full of delight at his appreciation. He did not know what had changed in that regard, but something had.

Just as somewhere along the way he'd lost the privilege of using the term *agape mou*. Oh, she never told him not to call her his love. She didn't do that anymore, make demands, or argue. She just winced every time he used the words, so he'd stopped doing it. She didn't seem to mind *yineka mou*, referring to her as his wife, his woman seemed acceptable. So, he found himself using that instead.

They made the helicopter trip to his childhood home in silence, which was not unexpected. Unless they wore headsets, hearing one another above the sound of the rotors was impossible without shouting. There had been a time she would have curled into his side, and they would have communicated with their eyes, if not their bodies. He did not remember the last time she'd offered that kind of open affection outside the bedroom.

Married friends had warned him that things changed naturally as a marriage settled into life's routines. He'd thought his would be immune, but even being wrong did not make him regret making this woman his wife.

Their ride from the helipad on top of the Kristalakis Building to the home where he'd grown up in the northern Athens suburb of Ekali went without incident and they arrived spot on time. Of course.

His mother greeted them both with the traditional kiss to both cheeks, though she showed respect for Pollyanna's makeup by kissing the air. Pollyanna returned the gesture, her expression perfectly contained. Not like the hothead he'd first married, who'd had a terrible time not showing the antipathy she'd developed for his mother on her expressive features.

Those features were never anything but serene now.

Except in bed.

In bed, Pollyanna still showed all the passion she ever had, with one exception. She never reached for him first.

He didn't recall when that changed, wasn't sure he would have noticed right away. Why should he? She always responded so beautifully to him when he initiated intimacy, but at some point he had become aware that she did not turn to him in the night. She did not reach across the bed to touch. She never kissed him with great enthusiasm and little concern for where they were as she'd used to do.

He'd accepted that kind of exuberance couldn't last in marriage. Her lack of enthusiasm was only in initiation, not the act, so he had nothing to complain about.

So, why did he still feel the loss so deeply?

"I see you're still making use of the stylist I suggested," his mother said to Pollyanna, in what should have been approval. So why did her words sound like a criticism?

Or was it that telltale wince that was barely there and then gone from his wife's lovely face?

"As you see," Pollyanna said in quiet self-deprecation.

Corrina, his new sister-in-law, who was usually all sunshine and smiles, was frowning at his mother, her expression not at all approving. "Polly doesn't need a stylist. Her natural style is perfect as it is."

His mother drew herself up in obvious affront, probably as much at the gentle rebuke as Corrina's use of Polly, which his mother thought far too common and had refused to use from their first meeting. Everyone called her Anna now, even him.

Though sometimes in bed, he still chanted Polly, when he was climaxing. The name he'd first come to know her by.

Alexandros looked to his brother, expecting him to subtly rein his wife in.

But Petros was smiling at Corrina in nothing less than approval. "As always, you are quite right, *agape mou*. She has never needed the stylists my brother insists on paying for."

The look Corrina gave Petros was nothing short of adoration. There was something about that look that bothered Alexandros, but he could not put his finger on what it was. It was a good thing that his newly married sister-in-law looked at her husband like he was a superhero. That was as it should be.

So why did Alexandros get a strange, unpleasant feeling every time he noticed it? He looked sideways at his own wife. She was not returning his regard.

No surprise there. She never looked at him unless good manners dictated she do so. She stood now, removed from the conversation like a statue in a museum.

"I do not expect to be taken to task in my own home," his mother said in freezing tones.

That didn't seem to impact Corrina at all.

Petros, on the other hand, wasn't so calm. Displeasure turned his expression dark and he snapped, "Giving Polly a compliment is not taking you to task. My wife is allowed to have a different opinion from you, and if you are not mature enough to accept that, perhaps we need to rethink these family dinners."

"Petros, how dare you talk to me that way?" their mother demanded, sounding utterly shocked.

"Oh, Mama, don't take on so," their younger, and unashamedly spoiled sister butted in. "You know how protective Petros is of his beloved wife. It's the way of the Kristalakis male. You remember how Papa used to be?"

As always, mention of her dead spouse brought a fragile smile to his mother's face, and she unbent enough to nod. "I suppose, but still, Petros, I am your mother."

His mother had fallen apart after his father's death. After losing both her parents only a year prior, he maybe should have expected her broken response to further loss. But he hadn't, and things had gotten very bad before Alexandros had taken action.

For a time, he had worried they would lose her to grief. They nearly had. She'd stopped bathing, stopped going out. In desperation, he had booked her into a luxury rest facility.

It had worked and she'd returned to the villa more herself, but Alexandros never forgot those dark days and how fragile of spirit his mother was under her society *grande dame* facade.

"And Corrina is my wife."

There could be no doubt in that room which woman came first in Petros's estimation. His mother looked furious again, and Stacia glared at their brother. "No one is denying that. We all love Corrina." Then Stacia shook her head, put an arm around her mother and said, "You can't be angry you raised him to be so much like Papa."

"No, I suppose not."

Stacia smiled. "Corrina and Anna are the luckiest women alive, being married to Kristalakis men. I'm sure no one will ever measure up for me. They are the most protective and considerate men on the planet. Right, Anna?"

Alexandros was surprised when his sister tried to bring his wife into the conversation. Even after five years, Stacia hadn't warmed up completely to his American bride. But he was shocked stupid by Anna's response.

"I wouldn't know, Stacia. I never knew your father." Pollyanna moved to take a seat in one of the armchairs, precluding him sitting beside her. She didn't use to do that either. Another barely there wince worried him. Was she having pain in her back and pelvis again with this pregnancy? "But Alexandros has never been the protective and considerate husband to me that Petros is to Corrina."

The words were so shocking that for a moment, his

usually facile brain froze in trying to understand them. She had not just said that his brother was a better husband than him.

Pollyanna's reply to his sister had been incomprehensible enough, but the tone in which she said it even more so. His wife did not sound angry. She did not even sound resigned. Pollyanna sounded like she simply didn't care that *he*, Alexandros Theos Kristalakis, did not measure up to his younger brother in the husband stakes.

Worse was yet to come as he took in the reactions of his family.

Stacia managed to look both offended and *satisfied* at the same time. His mother's expression showed offence and concern, but it was Corrina's reaction that struck him like a blow to his ego. She looked at Pollyanna with undisguised pity. And his brother?

Petros wasn't looking at Pollyanna at all; he was looking at Alexandros, and his expression was equal parts anger and disappointment.

It was not the type of look Alexandros was accustomed to receiving from *any* member of his family, but especially his younger brother.

Alexandros had a realization so stunning, it nearly took him out at the knees. His brother and his brother's wife thought *he* was a poor husband. Even more staggering, the flat tone of his wife, the absolute belief that tone imbued to her own words said she thought the same thing.

A discussion he'd had with his brother before Petros's marriage to Corrina came back to Alexandros now.

Alexandros gave his brother, Petros, a stern glance over the coffee they shared after a productive meeting with their top-level executives. "Is it really so much to ask that you put your honeymoon off for one week so you can attend this gala? You know how important it is to our mother."

"Yes." Petros's glare was more than stern; it showed a stubborn resolve Alexandros was not used to his brother turning on him. "If you think I'm making the same choices in my marriage you've made in yours, then you are wrong. I know Mama had a hard time after Papa died, but her feelings are *not* more important than the woman I have chosen to spend the rest of my life with. I will never put her desires ahead of Corrina's."

"Family requires sacrifice. We balance the needs of our wives with those of the rest of our family." It hadn't been easy for Alexandros to watch his mother and wife jockey for position in his life.

But ultimately he'd never doubted Polly's ability to hold her own and stand up for herself when it mattered.

There was no humor in Petros's laugh. "You mean like you balance *your* wife's needs against that of our mother and sister?"

"Precisely."

"No thank you. I would like my wife to still be in love with me five years from now."

"What the hell is that supposed to mean?"

"It means that I am not putting off my honeymoon to make our mother happy."

At the time, Alexandros had dismissed the dramatic implication of his brother's words. But they came back to haunt the eldest brother now.

Had Pollyanna stopped loving Alexandros? She still responded to him in bed like a woman in love. Or a woman in lust. But love? It wasn't an emotion he'd been particularly worried about when they first got together. He'd called her *agape mou* but had rarely told her he loved her, and she'd never pressed for declarations of that nature. Not even when he proposed.

He'd taken that as more proof of how well suited they were.

Alexandros had said the words the first time when their daughter was born, and had given her an eternity ring to remind her of the sentiment when he did not say it.

Looking back, he realized she'd responded in kind but not with the kind of enthusiasm she'd said the words in the beginning. And he could not remember the last time *she'd* told *him* she loved him.

He thought, that like him, she realized they did not need the words.

"How can you say something like that?" his mother was saying with ringing censure.

Pollyanna tilted her head, like trying to understand the question. "Surely there is no reason for me to lie? There cannot be a single person in this room that harbors any illusions in regard to my place of priority in Alexandros's life."

She spoke like she meant what she said, like she couldn't understand *why* his mother had taken offence, why Alexandros might take offence. Then as if she had not said anything inflammatory at all, she turned to Petros and asked, "Have you and Corrina decided to stay in the Athens apartment for now?"

And his brother answered, pulling his wife into the discussion. Apparently, they were going to stay in the apartment. That was another difference between Petros and Alexandros.

His younger brother had moved into one of two penthouse apartments at the top of the Kristalakis Building when he graduated university and took up his first position in the family business.

He and Corrina had opted for her to move in there with him after their wedding, rather than back into the more spacious family home Alexandros had not moved out of until he bought the country villa he and Pollyanna lived in now.

Generations of their family had lived in the huge luxury villa together since his second great-grandfather had bought it for his new wife.

"But won't that be limiting once you start your family?" his mother asked.

Petros shrugged. "We're in no hurry to have babies, but when we do, we'll decide if we want to find a house in Athens, or move to the country like Alexandros did."

"We certainly enjoy our weekends at your villa," Corrina said to Pollyanna with a smile. "Though I'm sure it's as much the company as the location."

Pollyanna returned Corrina's smile with more warmth than he'd seen all evening.

He'd noticed that his brother had not said like Alexandros *and Pollyanna* did, because she hadn't had any say in their move, had she? Alexandros had seen how unhappy his wife was living with his mother, so he'd broken with generations of family tradition and bought them a house. And had it decorated.

His mother had assured him that surprising her with the fait accompli would delight his wife, who was not exactly inclined toward interior decor.

Pollyanna had *not* reacted with rapturous delight at the news they would be living in the country and he would be commuting to work in the city.

In fact, their argument about where they were going to live was the last big dustup he could remember with his then-volatile wife. He'd thought she'd finally settled into her place as the wife of a billionaire, had accepted he had her best interests at heart.

But that settling in had come with a cost that he was only now beginning to truly appreciate.

"Alexandros did not put off having children," his mother said in clear disapproval of his brother's stance in that regard.

Corrina looked ready to say something, but then shook her head and pressed her lips firmly together.

"What were you going to say?" Alexandros asked, still reeling from the knowledge his sister-in-law pitied his wife in her choice of husbands.

"It's not important."

"This is family. You should be able to speak your mind."

The scoffing sound that came from his wife's direction was surprising only in that she'd stopped making commentary on his family a long time ago. He'd thought her attitude toward his mother and sister had changed.

Had Pollyanna simply given up on trying to get him to see her point of view?

Corrina gave him a wary look. "I was only going to point out that if pregnancy was as difficult for you as it is for your wife, you might actually have waited to have children."

"That is a ridiculous thing to say," his mother censored. "It is a woman's lot to deal with the more difficult aspects of bringing children into the world. That does not make my son selfish for expecting his wife to give him heirs."

"My *wife* did not say it made my brother selfish." Petros sounded good and furious now, not merely annoyed with their mother, but pissed enough he would leave.

Unsurprisingly, it was Alexandros's wife who stepped in to smooth the waters. She was very good at that. "I love being a mother," Pollyanna said directly to Corrina. "I knew what I was in for when I agreed to have a second child."

His wife gave a serene facsimile of her genuine smile and looked at his mother now. "I know you don't mean to criticize either Corrina or Petros for their wish to wait a while before having children."

"No, of course not," his mother agreed.

Though even Alexandros was aware her words had certainly sounded like criticism.

Petros didn't look any more convinced than Alexandros felt, but Corrina looked more relaxed.

She smiled at Pollyanna. "You're a brilliant mother."

"Thank you. Helena is the joy of my life."

There had been a time when she had claimed that he and their marriage were the joy of her life, but he couldn't remember the last time she'd said anything similar either.

Dinner was announced then, precluding any further tense discourse.

Not merely because of the change of venue but because his wife did as he realized she always did and made every effort to steer the conversation in less volatile directions. As he sat there mulling over predinner discussion, he was still aware of how many times Pollyanna did not react to what were clearly pointed barbs from his mother or his sister.

Had it always been like this and he ignored it in favor of family peace?

It was past ten o'clock when they got in the back of the limo for their ride to the helipad so they could return home.

Alexandros had been stewing all evening and barely waited for the door to shut them into seclusion before saying, "I can't believe you told my family you don't think I'm an attentive husband."

The laugh his comment startled from his wife was anything but amused. "Are you trying to claim that you are?"

"When have I ever neglected you?" he demanded in a driven tone. "Would you look at me when we're talking?"

She lifted her head, her blue eyes shadowed by fatigue not anger. "When haven't you?" she asked.

"I am not a neglectful husband."

"If you say so." She let her head fall back against the headrest and closed her eyes.

"It's not even worth arguing with me over?"

"I don't know if you've noticed, but there are very few things I find worth arguing with you over anymore, Alexandros."

When she used to argue about everything, screaming when he would not listen. She hadn't even argued over her refusal to bring their daughter to the family dinners.

Pollyanna had simply pointed out in a very reasonable tone that since Helena was usually in bed by the time they ate, keeping her up was not conducive to the baby's well-being. She'd added that Athena and Stacia were welcome to visit during little Helena's awake hours.

She hadn't mentioned his brother because Petros had made an effort to spend time with his sister-in-law and then his niece from the very beginning, the only person in Alexandros's family who had accepted Pollyanna's joining the family without any reservations. He and Corrina now came to Villa Liakada to visit once a week, frequently opting to stay the weekend and fly back into Athens on Sunday evening with Alexandros and Polly for the family dinner.

Petros and Corrina had made their visit midweek this time around however.

Though their daughter, Helena, was now three, she was still too young to be kept up. Alexandros and Pollyanna had yet to revisit the issue.

"Why didn't you ever suggest that my mother change our family gatherings to the midday meal so our daughter could be included?" he asked.

"Why would I? I have no sway with your mother. She's not my family." The last was said with absolute certainty.

But it was not true. His mother *was* her family. Only clearly, Pollyanna did not see it that way. Had Pollyanna refused to accept the connection, as he had always assumed, or did that lack lay at his mother's door?

Had he made too many concessions to his mother because of her emotional fragility and too many demands of his wife because of the strength he knew she possessed?

Emotional self-analysis was not something he was comfortable with, but he was beginning to see that so much he had taken for granted was not as he believed it to be.

"Did you expect me to make the suggestion?" he asked her, trying to understand a relationship he had thought he had figured out perfectly.

"No."

"Why not?"

"Did you make it?" she asked wearily.

"No." He had never even thought of changing a long-standing tradition until just that moment and was a little ashamed of that fact.

Not only would his daughter have gotten to spend more time with her *yia-yia*, but the more casual setting of lunch would have been easier on his wife. Though she'd never said so.

"Then?" she prompted, with little interest lacing her tone.

Having no answer and not even sure why he'd brought it up, he admitted, "I don't like you telling my brother he's a better husband than me."

"I would never presume to comment on how good a husband your brother is."

"You said he was more attentive and considerate than I am."

"If those are the traits by which you measure good or bad, you might take issue, but we both know you don't."

"What is that supposed to mean?" he demanded, noticing as if from outside himself that his voice was rising.

She didn't seem to care he was practically shouting, not bothering to open her eyes or look at him again. "If you wanted to be attentive, you would be. If you wanted to be protective, you would be. If you wanted to be considerate, you would be." She stopped, thought. "Maybe. Being considerate means noticing how the decisions you make affect others, and I think you're really bad at that."

"I make decisions that affect thousands of people all the time."

"Yes."

"And you don't think I care how they are affected?"

"No."

Just that. No. Not a reason why or a maybe. Just *no* and he knew she meant it.

She had no idea that he did his best to maximize jobs and keep people employed in jobs they *wanted*, even if it couldn't always be in the same company, or even country. And she assumed those kinds of considerations never made it past his ruthless need to also maximize profits.

"I can be considerate," he informed her, wondering how she'd missed his efforts in their marriage.

Had he really got it so wrong? For *five* years?

"To your mother, maybe," Pollyanna acknowledged without missing a beat. "But even as much as you spoil Stacia, I wouldn't say you are particularly considerate of her feelings or desires when they conflict with what you want or the way you think things should be done."

"Is this another argument where you lament the fact I won't always take your part against my mother?" Even as he asked the question, he tried to remember the last time they had had that disagreement and knew it was years past.

"No. I wasn't aware we were arguing at all." She sighed, still not opening her eyes. "Is there a reason for this conversation? Only I'm really tired."

"I forgot. I'm not worth arguing with."

"Alexandros, what exactly do you want me to say here?"

"That I'm not a bad husband," he blasted her.

Finally. Finally, her head snapped round, her eyes opening to flash at him with anger he remembered but had not seen in too long.

"Alexandros, I am six months pregnant and the mother of a very active toddler. Even without all the committees you insist I chair or participate in, I would be exhausted. Not just tired. Exhausted." And suddenly she looked it, her usual vibrancy so muted as to almost be extinguished.

She placed her hand protectively over her baby bump. "I am making new life inside me and I still suffer from nausea. It hurts to sit in any but the most comfortable chairs, hurts to walk and stand. Just like with my last pregnancy. But still you *insist* I suffer through a stylist's ministrations so I can attend these unpleasant family dinners, which require an uncomfortable fifty-minute helicopter ride each way."

"I did not realize it was such a struggle for you." But he should have.

Damn it. He should have.

"Of course you didn't, and if you had? You would not have cared. Never once, in our entire five years of marriage, have you *ever* made a decision with my happiness, or even my well-being at the forefront of your mind. A bad husband? No, you're not a bad husband. You're a *terrible* husband."

In receipt of those indictments, he was shocked stupid and silent for several long moments.

"If I'm so awful, why have you stayed married to

me?" he asked finally, a wholly unexpected fear that one day maybe she *wouldn't* taking root inside him.

He'd realized long ago that the material benefits of being married to a billionaire were not the perks he thought they would be for her. So, what kept her married to a man she considered a total failure as a husband?

"You're just now asking yourself that?" She sighed. "We made promises before God, and I won't just ignore those promises in favor of an easy out. We also have a child together. From the moment of conception, I stopped making decisions based solely on my own happiness."

He had no doubt she spoke the truth on both counts, but those reasons for his wife staying married to him were not exactly good for his ego.

"So you'll stay married to me no matter what?" That didn't jibe with the woman he knew his wife to be under the placid facade.

"No, not no matter what."

"What would make those vows invalid?" he was driven to ask, a nameless dread telling him that he was on the thinnest ice when he hadn't even realized he'd stepped out onto the frozen lake.

"Abuse. Infidelity."

"And that is all I have going for me? I don't abuse you and I'm not unfaithful."

"Pretty much, yeah." She sighed. "And you're good in bed," she added as if forced to do so. "You are not a selfish lover."

Just selfish in every other way.

He had no words to respond to that statement.

CHAPTER TWO

THEY HAD ARRIVED at the helipad, and for the first time ever, Alexandros was relieved to have a confrontation interrupted because he literally did not know where to go from here.

He watched his wife scoot to get out of the car and really noticed for the first time just how tired she was. Why hadn't he noticed before? Those bruises under her eyes had been there before they left the house. The way she moved more slowly than normal—that had been there too.

He cursed and then reached in to lift her out into his arms and carried her to the helicopter. She didn't fight him. In fact, she gave him the biggest shock in an evening of shocks when she relaxed into him and simply let him take her weight.

Was it a sign that on some primal level she still trusted him? Or was she simply *that* exhausted?

When they got into the helicopter, he shrugged out of his dinner jacket and then pulled her into his arms, putting it around her like a blanket. Again, she didn't fight him, but relaxed into him, falling asleep almost immediately.

Okay. *That* exhausted.

She did not wake on the flight home, nor when he lifted her from the helicopter and carried her inside.

When he reached their bedroom, Alexandros undressed his wife for the first time since meeting her *without* plans to have sex. Not that the sight of her body didn't turn him on. It *always* turned him on, but he wasn't such a monster he couldn't see how much she needed her rest.

No matter what she chose to believe, he did care about her well-being. Of course he did. She was his wife. And though he rarely said the words, he loved her.

He carefully removed the pins from her hair and fetched makeup wipes from their en suite in order to do what he'd never done before. He gently removed all traces of the makeup he knew she did not like to wear.

So, why did she wear it?

Because he'd made it clear he expected her to look the part of the wife of Alexandros Kristalakis, one of the most powerful men in Greece, if not the world.

He'd thought he was helping her fit into a world she had no experience of, but he couldn't help wondering how much help his advice couched as demands had really been.

Alexandros might be singularly obtuse to her feelings like she accused him, but he'd noticed that while she did the charity work he insisted was part of being his wife, she chose to support charities that his mother did not. His wife had put the power of his purse behind children's charities and those that served the marginalized, charities that did not have the cachet of those his mother supported.

In five years, his wife had built her own circle of friends and interests, and while those circles might overlap his and that of his influential family, they were not encompassed by them. Were in fact, he realized, as far removed from them as she could get without removing herself completely from his sphere of influence.

He finished preparing his wife for bed and then slid her lovely, pregnant body under the sheet and summer-weight duvet. She didn't shift until he joined her in the bed, forgoing the call to China he'd meant to make. He put his arm over her and tugged her close, the feeling that he was on the verge of having her ripped right from his arms too strong to ignore.

"Andros," she whispered against his chest in her sleep.

He went rigid at the name he hadn't heard in years, not even during lovemaking. Then without even consid-ering it, he was turning and facing her, gently shaking her shoulder. "Why don't you call me Andros any-more?"

"Andros was the man I fell in love with," she said in a voice that sounded more asleep than awake.

"And who is Alexandros?"

"The man I married." She made a snuffling sound and turned in her sleep. Away from him.

Alexandros wrapped his body around his wife, his entire perception of his life going through a painful metamorphosis.

Polly woke warm and relaxed, feeling better than she had all week despite the way the night before had ended.

She had no memory of undressing or taking off her makeup the night before, but she slept naked, the way her husband liked her, with no day-old mascara clumped on her lashes when she blinked her eyes open.

Polly was alone in the bed. Nothing new about that, but the single yellow rose on her husband's pillow was.

She picked it up and automatically brought it to her nose to sniff as she read the note he'd left with the flower on her pillow.

Good morning, *agape mou*.

Nothing life altering in those four words, except it was the first time in their relationship that Alexandros had written a personal note to her. He didn't do cards for holidays or anniversaries, or even her birthday. He did big, extravagant gifts that touched her less than a simple card would have done. Money was easy for Alexandros.

Sentiment would have been harder.

He did texts and sometimes phone calls, but since she stopped replying immediately or picking up the phone every time his number showed, those instances had become less common.

She went to find her daughter, knowing the little girl would be up soon if Helena was not already. They breakfasted together like they usually did, Polly answering her precocious three-year-old's many and often unexpected questions. Today's topic was pandas, culminating in an altogether to be expected request to visit the zoo.

The thought of walking the long pathways at the zoo with a rambunctious toddler did not appeal, but they could take the nursery maid with them, so Polly said, "Maybe, darling, but not today."

"Okay, Mommy."

Polly's phone buzzed with a text and she checked

it, startled when it was Alexandros inquiring how she was feeling.

She shot off a quick reply—Fine—and went back to talking the merits of different habitats at the zoo with her daughter.

A second text buzzed seconds later.

Do not say you are fine when you are not. Are you still exhausted?

She stared down at the phone in consternation. Since when was she not supposed to say she was fine when she wasn't? Alexandros didn't do drama. He didn't do anything that interfered with his well-ordered, fully business-oriented life.

Why are you asking? Is there something you want to add to my schedule?

That was the only thing she could think would have prompted the unprecedented text. But then why hadn't he contacted her social secretary? She'd hired Beryl the first year of their marriage, when Polly had realized that she needed a buffer between herself and the in-laws from hell. And that chances were, her husband was never going to be that buffer.

From an old elite Athens family that had fallen on hard times, Beryl was the perfect person to arrange social occasions with Alexandros's family and the rest of Athens society. Her efficiency also made it possible for Polly to fulfill her responsibilities as the wife of a billionaire and still be the kind of mom she'd always determined to be.

She sent another quick text off to Alexandros.

Just text Beryl. She has my calendar.

Which of course Alexandros knew, but Polly was thrown for a loop and reacting.

Her phone rang and she was surprised to see it was Alexandros.

"Hello."

"I'm not trying put more on your schedule, *yineka mou*. I was simply trying to find out if you are feeling any better this morning. You were well and truly exhausted last night."

"I'm pregnant. It comes with the territory."

"But having to get dressed up to attend an unpleasant weekly family dinner doesn't help, does it?"

Was he expecting her to apologize for saying that? She wasn't going to. If he didn't like the truth, he should not ask for it. Or better yet, he should make a different truth.

But she'd given up on that happening when she was pregnant with Helena.

"I will be home for lunch," he said into the silence between them.

"Why?" she asked in surprise.

"To see my wife and daughter."

She didn't say, *But you just saw me last night*, because though that was true, their daughter would be thrilled to see her beloved papa.

"We'll see you then. Only if you want me to wait lunch for you, that's fine, but Helena goes down for her nap at one o'clock."

If he was expecting their daughter to skip her nap

to play happy families, Polly was going to have to re-arrange their schedule if she didn't want to deal with a super cranky toddler for the rest of the day.

"I will be there by noon."

"All right."

The sound of a helicopter landing at five minutes to twelve brought Polly's attention up from the plans Beryl had given her to go over for an upcoming fund-raiser. Helena was coloring at her little desk beside her mother's in the room Polly had appropriated for her use after moving into the mansion.

Besides the nursery, it was the only room that had any stamp of Polly's personality and preference for comfort and warm colors in it. The rest of the mansion they called a home looked like a high-end modern hotel. Even their bedroom felt like she should be calling for a late checkout on the rare occasions she slept in.

"That will be Papa. Shall we go meet him?" Polly put her hand out to her daughter.

"Papa is here?" Helena squealed, jumping to her feet.

Alexandros was crossing the lawn from the heli-pad when they got outside, a big smile on his face for his daughter. Helena pulled away from Polly and ran to him, her papa lifting the little girl and giving her a hug and kiss while listening with rapt attention to her baby chatter.

The sight of the super virile man holding the little girl made Polly's heart clench like it always did. This man might not be the husband she'd dreamed of, but he was *it* for her.

If she could have stopped loving him, she would have. But she'd learned that shutting off her emotions was a lot harder than pretending for the sake of her pride that she didn't have any.

Alexandros had wanted to know the night before why she had stayed married to him, and she'd withheld the most relevant answer. She had fallen head over heels in love with him five and a half years ago.

And she still loved him. He wasn't perfect, but there was so much about him to love.

It came out over lunch that Helena wanted to go to the zoo, but instead of looking at Polly like he expected her to tell him when that was going to happen, Alexandros gave her a worried frown. "Wouldn't that be taxing for you right now?"

She wanted to snap that everything was taxing for her in that minute, but Polly didn't do waspish comments anymore. She'd grown up. Or so she told herself.

So she shrugged instead. "I can hardly expect our daughter's life to go on hold simply because her mom is pregnant."

"If we had a nanny, she could take her."

It was an old argument. Polly had refused to hire a full-time nanny, preferring instead to have two different nursery maids working different shifts. Dora, a middle-aged widow, was on hand from six in the morning until two in the afternoon. And Hero, a local girl who had been attending online university while helping her parents on their farm, covered the hours from six to midnight.

Both had rooms in the mansion, and Polly was sure Hero found her studies much more manageable than she had as a farm laborer, especially as Helena was usually asleep by eight.

And neither woman had primary responsibility for

Polly's child. Polly was and always would be a hands-on, dedicated mom. "Dora could take her, come to that," she told her husband. "But I'm Helena's mom. Our outings together are important."

"And when you are feeling better, you will be able to go on them again," he said, his tone oh, so reasonable.

"If this pregnancy is like my last one, my discomfort isn't going anywhere."

"Call it what it is, pain. And since I realized you were suffering from it again, I've researched possible remedies."

"I am not taking painkillers." They'd had that discussion when she was pregnant with Helena, and Polly had thought he'd agreed with her.

"Naturally not, but have you considered chiropractic and acupuncture? I have the name of a reputable clinic staffed by two doctors that have only rave reviews from their patients."

"You want me to try alternative medicine? *You* do?" Mr. Conservative, only the Greek way is the best way, and only the really rich Greek way of doing things met even that mark?

"It is not alternative medicine. It is perfectly valid holistic medicine. Thousands of years of success cannot be discounted as merely alternative."

"Who are you and what have you done with Alexandros Kristalakis?"

He laughed, the sound booming and masculine and altogether alluring.

But she hadn't been joking. She really didn't understand what was going on. "How did you even think to look for that clinic?"

"I told you, I did some research."

"Because you realized I was in pain?"

"I wish I had realized sooner, or that you had told me."

"But why would I tell you?" she asked in honest bewilderment.

Anytime she'd complained during her first pregnancy, he either asked his mother to advise Polly, which had never been a pleasant experience, or he'd quoted some lowering thing his mother had said. To this day, Polly herself wasn't sure if Athena said the things she did to undermine Polly, or because she really believed them.

Athena was of a different generation, not to mention a completely different socioeconomic background.

The worst had been when Alexandros had fallen back on his standby that women had been enduring the inconveniences of pregnancies since the beginning of time. He always couched it with how strong and resilient Polly was, so of course she would be fine.

Only she hadn't been fine. First, she'd be nauseated to the point of throwing up several times a day, all day long for the first four months. Then a month of relative bliss and then the pain in her pelvic floor had started, followed quickly by lower back pain and finally pain in both hips had stacked on top of that for her final month with a return of her nausea.

This time around, the nausea had clung on past the fourth month, but she was no longer throwing up, so that was an improvement.

He stared at her like she was the one being incomprehensible, but when had her husband ever invited her to share her complaints with him? He was a dynamic workaholic who powered through lack of sleep and physical infirmity with a strength of will that used to intimidate her.

Because she'd felt the need to be worthy of that kind of dynamism. She didn't anymore.

Polly accepted that while that was who her husband was, it was not her.

And she accepted the fact that he expected those around him to deal with their own challenges. So, she did, even if she gave herself more of a break than he ever would have done.

Or tried to anyway, within the parameters of her job description.

Socially conscious wife to Alexandros Kristalakis.

"Perhaps because if you had told me, I would have made changes sooner."

Change would be a fine thing. "What changes?" she asked anyway, wondering what he considered concessions made to her condition.

"I have informed my mother and sister that until further notice, our once a week family get-togethers will happen here and they will be lunches, not dinners."

"What? Why?" Did she *want* to host the family meals? Wouldn't that just give Athena, and more likely Stacia, even more reasons to criticize Polly?

But she could not deny that a lunchtime get-together would be much easier for Polly to manage from both a physical and schedule perspective.

"It is a change that should have happened when you first got pregnant. I forget that other people do better with more sleep than I get, and my pregnant wife should be getting even more sleep than her usual." He gave her a self-deprecating smile that sort of took her breath away.

Her husband did not *do* self-deprecating.

"You don't believe that. You don't believe in giving in to infirmity."

His smile slid away to be replaced by an expression that almost looked hurt. "Am I really that arrogant? That lacking in compassion?"

"Yes," she answered immediately and without a shred of desire to lie.

His strong features showed consternation. "I am sorry you believe that, but trust me when I tell you that your pain and discomfort *do* affect me."

"Since when?"

"Always."

"But before…" She let her voice trail off, not sure it was worth getting into.

His handsome mouth firmed. "Not worth discussing?" he asked silkily. "But I will answer your implied question. The last time you were pregnant, I was in the middle of a takeover bid from a conglomerate that wanted my flagship company. I was not as focused on you as I should have been, which was why I asked for my mother's help."

Polly didn't mask her expression fast enough to hide what she thought of his mother's *help*.

He smiled ruefully. "Just so. I accept that she was not the comfort to you I thought she would be."

Appreciative of that insight, belated though it might be, Polly went back to what else he'd revealed. "But surely no takeover bid could have been any real threat."

"One thing you will learn in business. No matter how big you are? Someone is always bigger, if only temporarily. I'd made some risky moves, not realizing they were waiting for just such an opportunity. I was too focused on business, and when you told me the difficulties you were having with your pregnancy, my mother assured me you were fine. It was all very normal. Your doctor confirmed that."

"It was normal, if not easy for me to deal with." And she'd really wanted his support, not his mother's repressively traditional advice.

"I really thought Mama would help you through the difficulties of pregnancy while I worked seven days a week to keep my business."

"Your mother *help me*?" Polly asked in disbelief, even as she appreciated he hadn't just ignored her for business as usual. And he'd believed she was okay because maybe that was what he needed to believe while his attention was directed elsewhere.

It put her last pregnancy in a different light, but it didn't appreciably change how she saw her husband's attitude to her. Because whatever the cause, even pregnant, Polly had not been anything like his primary concern.

"I did not appreciate how old-fashioned her views on pregnancy were," he acknowledged with unexpected candor.

Even oblique criticism of his mother was not something she was used to from Alexandros.

He was very protective of the older woman. He'd once shared how close to losing her he'd felt he'd come after the unexpected death of his father.

The Kristalakis patriarch had only died a little over a year before she and Alexandros met. She'd wondered sometimes if that was what had driven Alexandros's uncharacteristic impromptu marriage proposal.

"Or how much she *enjoyed* my discomfort."

He frowned. "I'm sure that is not true."

And with that, they reached the end of any honest dialogue about his mother and her attitude toward Polly.

Polly didn't bother to argue her viewpoint. She'd learned there was no advantage to it. He didn't hear criticism of his precious mother.

And honestly? Polly wasn't sure Athena *had* enjoyed her pain. It had seemed like it though, all mixed up with Athena's and Stacia's efforts to undermine Polly's place in Alexandros's life.

Regardless, Polly would not allow a few unexpected moments of understanding on his part lull her into thinking Alexandros had changed in any significant way.

This refrain, in different guises, was an old one. Athena Kristalakis had been furious with her son marrying an American nobody instead of one of the beautiful Greek socialites she'd been pushing at him for years.

Under the pretext of friendship, Athena had drawn proverbial blood over and over again in her campaign to send her unwanted daughter-in-law packing. She and her daughter Stacia had done their best to make Polly feel like the outsider she was, making sure those in their circle treated her with the same disdain they did.

Athena had even changed Polly's first name! Calling her Anna, without asking for Polly's approval. Which she would *not* have given.

Anna was *not* Polly's name and she never thought of herself that way. However, as time went on, Polly had allowed her *Anna* persona to develop. The Anna facade stood between her and any real interaction with her detractors, and most of the time, even with her husband anymore.

"Your silence does not signify agreement," he said as if just figuring that fact out.

"No, it does not." It never had.

"It is your way of telling me you can't be bothered to argue any longer."

"Maybe." She was reeling.

He'd gone from stone dense to insightful literally overnight, and Polly didn't know how she felt about that.

"I think my mother has almost as much ground to make up with you as I do."

Suddenly, Polly had her own insight.

Her husband was terribly competitive. And last night she had inadvertently triggered his need to prove he was the better husband between himself and his younger brother.

News flash—that would require something Alexandros simply could not give her.

His love.

"I'm beginning to realize just how often you use silence as its own answer," he said in a tone she found difficult to interpret.

"You used to tell me off all the time for disagreeing with you so often."

"Be careful what you wish for—isn't that how the saying goes?"

"Are you saying you *want* me to argue with you?" She didn't buy it. Not for a single second.

"I want you to think it's worth it."

"It's a goal to shoot for," she said with more facetiousness than she usually allowed herself with him.

His sardonic look said he recognized it. "You have an appointment with the chiropractor and acupuncturist the day after tomorrow," he said, changing the subject away from confrontation like he never did. "I would have arranged it for tomorrow, but you've already got your appointment with your OB."

"Wednesday? But I have committee meetings in Athens. Did you forget I was going to fly in on the helicopter with you?" Beryl had arranged it, as she always did when Polly needed to get into city.

Polly would come home in a car with a driver, usually after sharing lunch with her busy husband. It was one of those treats she looked forward to. Adult time during the day with Alexandros.

"There will be no more uncomfortable helicopter rides into Athens for the duration of your pregnancy." His tone said this was not one of those occasions he wanted her to think it was worth arguing with him.

Too bad! "But my charity work!" Work he'd insisted she had to do in order to fulfill her responsibilities as his wife.

"Can be done by someone else."

Like *her* efforts had no intrinsic value because she was the one making them? Thank you so much, husband! "What if there is no one else?"

"We will hire Beryl an assistant and she will take your place in committees, etc. After working for you so long, she knows your stand on things, what you would want to involve yourself in and what you would not." He reached across the table and took her hand. "Listen to me, *pethi mou*. You are too valuable to me to allow you to continue putting your health at risk. And while the work you do on behalf of children at risk and the marginalized is incredibly important, it is not more important to me than *you* are."

He was saying all the right things, but she wasn't believing them.

She couldn't afford to let herself go down that road again, where she thought he loved her, valued her and had married her for anything other than the untrammeled lust he felt for her body.

"While Beryl is invaluable to me, *she* is not the wife of a billionaire."

"But she has your ear, which means she influences your donation and spokesperson power. It will suffice for this season of your life."

Season? Did he mean beyond delivery of their second child? "I assume you've already spoken to Beryl about this change in her duties." He might make it sound like he'd just thought of hiring her social secretary an assistant, but Polly wasn't that naive.

Alexandros did not wait to act.

His hand squeezed hers. "Naturally, you are right. You know me well."

But did he know her? "Didn't you think that maybe you should have discussed some of these changes with me before you made them?"

"I saw a problem and I sought to fix it. What is wrong with that?"

"The problem is mine to fix."

"Only you weren't fixing it. You were running yourself ragged doing all the same old stuff."

She couldn't deny that. Polly had her own measure of pride and hadn't wanted to admit she wasn't physically up to the same schedule she'd always kept. "If you've hired a nanny behind my back, we are going to have some serious words," she warned him.

"It would almost be worth it to see you engaged

enough to actually argue with me, but that is not something I would do."

"You *want* me angry with you?" she asked. This was the second time he'd alluded to wanting that and she was trying to understand *why* suddenly he wanted her to revert to how she'd used to be.

Willing to argue every time she didn't agree with his autocratic view of the world. Angry with him more often than she'd ever wanted to be.

Because she kept expecting him to treat her like he loved her.

She didn't have those expectations any longer.

"No." Which did not surprise her. "I want you *real* with me, and I'm only just now realizing how long it has been since I saw the real Pollyanna. Only in the same way I have realized that there are an honored few that already do."

"What do you mean?"

"My brother. His new wife. The few you call friend and not acquaintance."

He'd left off her family, but maybe that was because he realized bringing them up would only point out how differently her parents and siblings treated Polly to how his own mother and sister did. "None of them call me Anna."

And at its most basic level, that was the dividing line.

"So, all I have to do is call you Pollyanna to get back into the charmed circle?" he asked in that seductive tone he usually reserved for the bedroom.

Heat climbing her cheeks at her body's instant reaction to it, she said, "I don't know what circle you're talking about."

But she did. He meant the people she trusted, including those few she'd learned she could rely on since moving to Greece.

Her husband, she had learned *not* to trust.

"Yes, you do."

"Yes, I do," she admitted.

"I call you Anna."

"Yes."

"You do not like it."

"It is not my name."

"It is a nickname."

"That your mother finds more acceptable than my real name. Yes, I know."

"You have never asked me to call you Pollyanna instead."

She shook her head. Was he rewriting history now? "That is not true."

He stared at her, his mouth open to refute her words, but then he must have remembered. Because he went oddly pale. "You told me Anna was not your name and you would prefer if I would not use it."

"But your mother had made it clear how very lowbrow she found my real name."

"So, I called you Anna around her."

"Not just around her."

He winced in acknowledgment. "I slipped once too often and realized I needed to use it all the time, for consistency."

The other option of course would have been for him to *never* use it. For consistency. And because Polly had made it clear that was what she wanted. But then, when had Polly's wants, or even needs, ever trumped his mother's? Never, that was when.

Their daughter demanded her father's attention right

then, and Polly was grateful for it. She was done with this weird walk down memory lane.

No one could change the path their marriage had taken, because she'd realized way too late that she'd married a man programmed to hurt her.

Because, despite a few claims to the contrary, usually when she'd done something that made him really happy, like giving birth, he did not love her.

No man who loved her would treat her the way that Alexandros had since their marriage and her move to Greece. The very fact he'd insisted on moving into his family home, one they had had to share with the two wicked witches, showed just how little her feelings had mattered to him.

He knew from the beginning that Athena had wanted him to marry an entirely different type of woman. It had taken Polly longer to see the contempt behind the smile.

Even so, Alexandros would be *so* annoyed if he knew she thought of his mother and sister in those terms.

But Polly's thoughts were her own and even her *had to be in charge* husband could not police them.

They put their daughter down for her nap together, and Polly enjoyed the family togetherness so much, moisture burned the back of her eyes.

"Are you all right?" he asked as they left their daughter's bedroom together.

"I'm fine." She didn't consider that two-word answer deception.

She simply said what he expected to hear.

Suddenly she found herself in his arms and being carried past the staircase that would have taken them back downstairs, down the hall and to *their* bedroom.

"It's the middle of the day, Alexandros!"

"When has that ever stopped me?"

It was true that some weekends they utilized the time during their daughter's naps to enjoy marital intimacy, but since he was never home during the day during the week, and not always on the weekends, it was something very new.

"Don't you have to get back to the office?" she asked in wonder as he laid her down on their bed, his expression harsh with need that hadn't been there a moment ago.

Or maybe it had been and she just hadn't let herself notice it.

"The office can wait." He removed his jacket and tie in rapid succession, his nimble fingers already working the buttons of his shirt open.

She gasped, her shock was so great at that unprecedented statement.

CHAPTER THREE

ALEXANDROS IMPATIENTLY TUGGED his shirt over his head with only the cuffs and a few buttons undone. Shock turned to passion as the body she loved touching so much was revealed to her hungry gaze.

He unhooked his leather belt and didn't even bother taking it from the loops as he usually did before undoing his slacks to push them down his hips.

"They're going to get wrinkled like that."

"Do you care?" he asked lazily.

She shook her head, her gaze glued to his now-naked body.

"I love the way you look at me. In the bedroom." There was something strange in his expression she couldn't read though. Like something about what he'd said bothered him.

Polly leaned up on her elbows, confident in this, as she was in no other area of their relationship. In this area, there could be no denying they were entirely simpatico.

While she no longer believed he loved her, the joining of their bodies was *still* making love because of her feelings for him. And she did believe he felt affection for her.

It wasn't all the amazing sexual compatibility they'd shared since the first time they touched.

"You do it for me," she said cheekily but with a heated look she knew he wouldn't misinterpret.

"Tease me at your own peril," he warned.

But she wasn't worried. Polly reached down to tug at her dress, as if she was going to pull it off.

He leaped. Like literally leaped and took hold of her wrists. "No. That's mine."

"What is yours?" she taunted.

"Undressing you."

"I undress myself all the time."

"Not when I'm there to do it for you."

And that was true. Even when sex wasn't in the offing, her husband considered it his privilege to take her clothes off if he was around to do it. Whether it was to get ready for bed or to change for dinner didn't matter. He got a big charge out of it.

This time though, sex was definitely in the offing. It spiced the air around them, making it heavy with the mutual desire that had not dimmed in five years of marriage.

His sex rigid with need, he crossed the carpet to their bed. When he reached Polly, her husband tugged her to her feet and turned her around so he could slide the zip down on her dress, revealing curves that were exaggerated by pregnancy. He took his time peeling her dress down her arms and sliding it ever so slowly down her body.

"Now, who is teasing, Alexandros?" she asked, her tone breathy with desire.

"Your husband."

"You are that." She'd never denied it, for good or ill.

"And I always will be," he said with more force than finesse before cupping her breasts. "No one else will ever touch you like this."

"You're feeling possessive."

"Because you are mine."

"And you are mine," she reminded him. "We have matching wedding bands."

His hot mouth landed against the side of her throat, sending her thoughts splintering. Alexandros knew all her hot spots and seemed intent on visiting each one.

Somehow, she found herself naked on the bed, his head between her legs, his mouth driving her pleasure higher and higher. Two fingers pressed inside of her, rubbing against that inner bundle of nerves that made her scream with need.

She wanted him inside her. "Alexandros! Now!"

But instead of moving up her body, he suckled at her clitoris, and she came with a long scream she couldn't have held back with the best will in the world. He nursed her through aftershocks of pleasure until she was nearly sobbing with the pleasure that was not abating.

Only then did he shift up her body and press his hardness into the wet, slick, swollen opening of her body.

He pressed inside her, stretching her, filling her, giving her more and more pleasure. His initial thrusts were long and slow, and she could feel a second climax build impossibly fast.

This time when she came, he was with her, his own hoarse shout blending with her cries.

Afterward, he pulled her close, his body wrapped around hers completely.

She rubbed her head against his chest and kissed his hard muscle. "This is nice."

"Better than nice."

"Mind blowing."

"Better."

She yawned. "Mmm. I shouldn't be tired. I slept in this morning."

"But you are pregnant. You need your rest."

"If you say so."

"I do."

She didn't know how long he cuddled her, but she was dozing when he slid from the bed. "I need to shower and get back to Athens."

"Work waits for no man," she mumbled.

He laughed. "Perhaps not, but it waited this afternoon for my woman."

She smiled at him, reveling in the truth of that statement.

Polly fell asleep to the sound of him showering in the en suite, waking hours later to discover he'd given strict instructions for her not to be disturbed. Beryl had fielded calls, and Dora had agreed to remain overseeing Helena until Hero showed up. All organized by Polly's billionaire tycoon before he flew back to Athens.

Polly barely had time to make it to share dinner with their daughter, unsurprised when she got the message from the housekeeper that Alexandros had been held up in Athens and wouldn't be joining them. Helena asked, but wasn't upset when told her papa would see her to tuck her in later.

And he made it back in time to do so, so neither was Polly.

* * *

The next morning, Polly stopped in stunned silence when she realized her husband was sitting at the breakfast table with Beryl and Helena.

"I stayed to go to your obstetrician appointment with you." He sounded like he expected a medal for that.

"You said you didn't have time."

"When did I say that?"

"When I was pregnant with Helena."

"Things were different then."

"The takeover thing?" she asked.

He nodded, color scoring the masculine angles of his face. He didn't like thinking about that time any more than she did, if for very different reasons.

"Should I point out that I'm six months pregnant?"

"Things change."

Or he realized his brother would have been attending these appointments with Corrina from the beginning. Once again, he was competing in the husband stakes.

But since she'd always craved having him by her side for the doctor appointments, she simply said, "Okay."

He gave her a look she couldn't read, not that she tried very hard to do so. She was too busy getting her own suddenly chaotic thoughts into some kind of order.

She and Beryl went over her schedule for the day, and Polly realized Alexandros had meant business when he said he thought she was doing too much. He'd given Beryl instructions already to cancel things or go in Polly's place.

Polly didn't argue because, honestly? She was so tired today, she'd found it hard to get out of bed.

That wasn't unusual with this pregnancy, but she fought on, trying for normal.

* * *

Her OB's eyes widened and then narrowed when she realized that Polly's husband was with her.

They'd met only once before. When Polly had given birth to Helena. And it had not been a mutual admiration society then. Dr. Hope had been less than impressed when the father-to-be hadn't shown up until the final few minutes, having come after receiving the call he'd asked for.

One of the bodyguards, who was keeping tabs on what was happening in the birthing suite had let Alexandros know when it was time for Polly to start pushing.

Polly hadn't been alone though.

Alexandros had made it possible for her parents to come over from the States to stay the last two weeks of Polly's pregnancy. Her mom had been with her every minute and her dad in and out of her room during Polly's long labor.

Her father had returned to his job a week after Helena's birth, but her mom had remained another month. All at Alexandros's request, she reminded herself.

Considering how often her OB had suggested Polly cut back on her schedule, she probably should have expected Dr. Hope to tell Alexandros off for how tired Polly was, how she was clearly not being taken care of like she needed.

But the litany of reminders of how many ways in which Polly did *not* get the TLC she so desperately craved from her husband came as an unwelcome shock.

And in a wholly unexpected moment of out of control emotion, Polly ranted, "I don't know why everyone has to rub in the fact that my husband doesn't care enough about me to take even the most rudimentary care! Don't you think I know that? I'm doing the best I can."

Only maybe she wasn't. Maybe Polly needed to take a step back from her pride and let some of Alexandros's money do what he wasn't ever going to. Take care of her.

Dr. Hope looked pained. "I know *you* are, Polly." She cast a very pointed look at Alexandros.

"I do not think she was saying these things to rub it in as you say, *yineka mou*. She was saying them to me, to tell me what a selfish louse I've been, so maybe if enough people say it, I will *listen*."

"You're not a louse." Though sometimes she thought of him as a rat. Was that any different?

Polly turned her head away, because looking at her husband hurt right then, and she'd thought she'd come to terms with the limitations of their relationship. But he was rewriting the rules and she just didn't know why.

The rest of the visit went better with Alexandros asking all the questions any concerned husband and second time father-to-be might do. Dr. Hope unbent enough to answer every question patiently and without further condemnation.

Polly waited until they were in the car, the privacy window closed between them and the driver to ask, "Why are you being so nice to me? I just don't understand."

Then she had such a horrible, terrible thought, she couldn't breathe for a few seconds. The one area of her marriage she'd never worried about, was suddenly in doubt. The one thing she thought they got right. Maybe wasn't right anymore.

She didn't know why she'd never worried about it before. Maybe because he'd always been such an attentive lover. Maybe because he'd told her he abhorred infidelity and she had believed him. Maybe because she simply had never been able to imagine him as a cliché... The powerful tycoon philanderer.

But right now, with him acting so strangely, with her hormones and emotions all over the place from her pregnancy... Polly did wonder.

Sitting up straight, her body rigid with stress, she accused, "You've taken a pillow friend. That's what you Greek tycoons call them, isn't it? You've got a mistress and you don't want me to divorce you when I find out!"

"No." He looked like he wanted to laugh, but then seemed to all of a sudden realize she was very serious and how bad that was for their marriage. "No! Polly, you are the only woman I have touched intimately since our first date."

"Can I believe you?"

"Have I ever lied to you?"

"Yes." Pain of an entirely different kind racked her pregnant body. "Your sister warned me, but I thought she was talking nonsense. Trying to hurt me like she found such sport back when I used to let her get to me."

Alexandros could not believe what he was hearing. "I have failed spectacularly in the husband stakes, but I have *never* lied to you."

He could not even deal with what she was saying about how Stacia had treated her because the fact his wife did not trust him was instantly, glaringly obvious. This was not hormonal raving. Pollyanna did not believe him.

"You have," she disagreed.

"When?"

"When you asked me to marry you. You said you would do anything you had to to make me happy."

And clearly in her mind, he hadn't. "I thought giving you anything you wanted would make you happy."

"But you don't. Not the things that matter."

And finally, after five years, he might be starting to understand the distinction. "I'm working on it."

"But you lied then. You lied when you said you loved me."

"I did not lie. I just didn't understand what I needed to do to keep those words true. And I do love you."

She laughed like that was a great joke, only she didn't sound happy about it.

"You are my wife, by *my* choice. I am not lying." The words sounded hollow to his own ears as he realized just how stopped up the ears were they were falling on.

"A man does not treat a woman the way you've treated me when he's in love with her." Pollyanna sounded so certain in her own mind, so sure of her interpretation of the years of their marriage he knew denial would be useless.

He said it anyway. "A man too focused on his business and keeping peace within his extended family does."

A man still grieving the loss of his father and afraid of how close he'd come to losing his mother. Despite how much he wanted to fix what was broken, those words would not leave his lips. Alexandros had never been an emotionally vulnerable person.

It was not his nature.

It was not how his bigger-than-life father had taught him to be.

Unimpressed with the words he had managed to

utter, Pollyanna shrugged, turning her head away, and he knew the words again had fallen on deaf ears.

Or maybe they had been the wrong ones.

"I will change," he promised. Had already started changing, but he didn't expect her to trust that.

"Not on my account."

"Naturally on your account, but on mine too. I want what we had in the beginning."

"It's dead."

He didn't believe that, but clearly he hadn't just failed, he'd destroyed the fragile bonds of trust between them. All right. Okay. He'd taken over businesses that looked like they could never be revived. Some of those companies were his biggest earners now.

Let the rescue bid for his marriage commence.

When they were going over her schedule during breakfast on Wednesday, without another unexpected turn-up of Alexandros, Beryl told Polly not to worry about preparing for travel to her appointments with the doctors that Alexandros had set up.

Apparently, he had arranged for the appointments to take place at the mansion. There was already a massage table in the room off their personal gym, used by both her and Alexandros's personal trainers.

She wondered if Alexandros knew that Polly had stopped seeing her personal trainer the second month of her current pregnancy.

And then reminded herself she didn't care. Polly did what she had to in order to keep the peace, but no more. She'd built a life for herself in Greece that resembled the life he expected her to lead, but was not actually that life.

Except for a very superficial resemblance.

She was on charity committees, but not the flavor of the month, only the ones that really resonated with her. Most did not have the wherewithal to throw the glittery balls her mother and sister-in-law were so fond of. She'd made friends from those charities, not others from Alexandros's set, but normal people who cared enough to *sacrifice* time and money for causes they believed in.

Polly wore designer clothes and used a car and driver like Alexandros insisted. But she donated from her wardrobe twice yearly to charity auctions and only bought exactly what she would need for each season. Her walk-in closet never getting more than half-full. Her driver was a retired veteran with a disability that still allowed him to drive, but not a lot else to earn a living. Her car was the same one bought for her use the first year she married Alexandros.

Alexandros arranged for a new car for her every other year and she donated them for the use of the directors of the charities she knew needed them most.

Polly attended only the functions with her husband that she could not get out of and never gave up dinnertime with her daughter. She didn't fight about it; she simply didn't show up, and her husband had learned that time with their daughter was sacrosanct to Polly.

She wasn't unhappy. She loved being a mom. Loved her husband even if she knew he did not really love her. She *did* believe he was faithful. That moment in the car had been all pregnancy hormones, but he'd taken her seriously and that in itself had been a novel experience.

It had also cemented the belief she already had that he would not take a mistress.

No matter what Stacia said, Alexandros Kristalakis was not the type to keep a pillow friend.

He never broke his word on purpose. She didn't trust him, not because she thought he lied to get what he wanted but because he lied without meaning to, and that was in her view even more dangerous.

Polly knew that she and Helena were important to him, if not of utmost importance.

It was more than a lot of women had.

Maybe not all that Polly had wanted, or even believed she had when she agreed to marry the Greek tycoon, but not a bad life.

She looked across the table at her daughter and smiled. No, not a bad life at all.

Polly and Helena were in their saltwater pool, playing before lunch, when the sound of an arriving helicopter sent Polly's gaze winging upward.

It was Alexandros's helicopter, but she was sure he wasn't on it. It must be the transportation he'd arranged for the doctors. Her appointments weren't for another two hours though. Perhaps they needed time to set up?

She could have cut her time in the water with her daughter short, but there was a housekeeper to meet them and make sure they had what they needed.

Going back to the game intended to increase her daughter's comfort with putting her face under the water for swimming, Polly dismissed the arriving helicopter from her mind.

"Now, that is a beautiful sight." Humor and masculine appreciation filled her husband's voice.

Startled into immobility, Polly stared at the apparition standing on the pool deck. "Alexandros! What are you doing here?"

At the same time as she spoke, her daughter realized who was there and tried to leap away from her mother and toward her father, arms outstretched. "Papa!"

Six feet four inches of sartorial masculine gorgeousness leaned toward his daughter like the effect of salt water on his suit was of no concern.

Swooping Helena up as a maid strategically wrapped a towel around the little girl, he gave Polly a slashing grin. "I'm having lunch with my two favorite females and then working the rest of the day from home."

Like a landed fish, Polly stood there her mouth opening and closing, but with no words making their way past her lips. What was he doing here? His favorite females? Really?

"Not if your mom and sister are in the running." Polly snapped her mouth shut so hard, her teeth clicked.

She had not meant to say that. Hadn't made a comment like that since before Helena's birth. Not after he'd told her that the world did not revolve around her, that Polly would have to get over her *unnatural* jealousy of his family if their marriage was going to work.

Instead of getting angry as he used to do, her husband gave her another heart-stopping smile. "There is no competition, *yineka mou*. You are my wife and Helena is my daughter. No one is more important to me."

"Since when?"

But he just smiled again, shook his head and said, "Are you getting out? I thought Helena needed lunch so she could nap."

"She does, of course. We were only playing for ten more minutes."

"By all means, stay in the water. I like the view."

She looked down at her pregnancy-distended belly in the simple, but bright one-piece Polly had purchased for swimming in her final months before their baby's birth. What was there about this view for him to like? In *that* way? Because he was giving her a look over their daughter's shoulder that sent sensations she preferred to keep confined to their nights in bed together zinging through her body.

Regardless, the opportunity to swim a few laps without having to watch her daughter was all too appealing. Polly spent as much time in the pool as she could because it relieved the pressure in both her lower back and pelvis.

"If you're sure you're okay with her?" she asked him.

"Of course."

She didn't ask again, just turned and took a standing dive into the water, pushing for the other end of the pool.

Reveling in the freedom to swim unencumbered, Polly did a few leisurely laps before climbing out of the pool and grabbing a towel. She could have stayed in longer, but she couldn't stay away from the sweet tableau of father—suit jacket and tie now missing—and daughter—wearing her little terry cover-up—talking earnestly on one of the loungers closest to the pool edge.

Polly hated breaking it up, but she had to, or the sweet little girl would turn into a hungry, tired little terror. "Time to get dressed for lunch, poppet."

"But Mama…" Helena whined.

And Polly knew that tone. Definitely time for lunch and then nap.

"Come. Dora will help you dress while I help Mama."

"You're going to help me get dressed?" Polly asked delicately.

The heated look that came her way made her really wish they didn't have plans to eat with their daughter in a matter of minutes. *"Ne."*

Alexandros carried Helena inside and up the stairs, handing her off to Dora when they reached the landing and putting his arm around Polly to walk her to their bedroom.

"Why did you come home again today?" she asked breathlessly as they stepped inside the sanctuary.

He turned her around to face him. "Because I wanted to." Then he kissed her and she forgot the question and everything else. Just that quickly.

It was always like this. Polly could not resist the physical temptation of her husband. Not for a kiss, or for more. She never had been able to. Even more, she could not resist the emotional connection she felt to him during times of physical intimacy.

She knew it didn't go both ways or he could not spend as much time traveling as he did.

Because if it was up to Polly she would never have willingly spent a single night away from him.

He pulled her still-damp body right against him, letting her feel how quickly he had responded to the kiss. His hardness pressed against her and she wanted nothing more than to move to the bed so she could explore the hard male body she found such delight in.

Clever masculine fingers were peeling her swimsuit down her arms, exposing her breasts. Already beaded nipples tightened nearly painfully as the air brushed cool against wet skin.

He cursed before cupping her. "You are so beautiful."

"Pregnant," she said wryly. "Fat."

"Ypérochos, énkyos, dikos mou."

When they'd first married, she hadn't spoken any Greek, but she'd taken pains to learn. Because now she lived in Greece and it made communication easier, but mostly? Because he used Greek in bed and she'd wanted to know if he was saying he loved her. He didn't, but he did say stuff like this and it went straight to her heart.

Gorgeous. Pregnant. Mine.

"Yours." She had no problem admitting a truth she'd never been able to hide.

"Dikos mou. Gia pánta."

Forever? Yes, she supposed she was, but she didn't say it. "We have to get dressed," she said with real regret.

"I need to get *un*dressed and you need a shower," he corrected.

But she shook her head. "I'll have to shower after lunch. We're going to be late to the table as it is."

"We can phone down. Dora can see to Helena's lunch, *yineka mou.*"

"No. Our daughter is expecting us." Helena saw less of her father because of her sleep schedule than Polly saw of her husband. "It wouldn't be fair to her."

"And what of us? Is it fair to eat lunch when we want each other so much?"

"Didn't you once tell me that anticipation made it all the better?" He'd been talking about the nights they had to spend apart, when they both missed their physical intimacy. "If we're fast, we can share a shower after lunch and before my appointments."

"We will take as long as we need *after* lunch with our daughter."

And presumably the doctors could wait on the billionaire and his wife. Polly simply shook her head again. She could argue polite behavior after lunch too.

Helena was excitable over lunch, showing off for her papa and pushing to stay up and play rather than take her nap. "But I not tired, Mama."

"You need your rest, poppet."

"But Papa will be gone when I wakes up." Helena burst into floods of tears.

Before Polly could pull her cumbersome body to her feet to go around the table to comfort her daughter, Alexandros had said a not very nice word beneath his breath and leaped to his feet. He pulled their daughter into his arms and promised in both Greek and English that he *would* be there when she woke from her nap.

Helena's sobs only increased and Alexandros looked at Polly, his expression stunned.

"I don't know why she's crying like this," Polly admitted, hating that helpless feeling that was such a normal part of parenting.

Their daughter kept chanting *Mama*, but when Polly got up and came around the table to take her, she clung to Alexandros with all the strength in her little body.

"Come now, *agape mou*. This crying is not productive. Tell us what is wrong."

Polly covered the smile on her mouth at the business speak leveled at their three-year-old, but it was all she could do not to laugh.

"I don't want prod-i-vive," their daughter wailed.

That was it. Polly bust out laughing, and both father and daughter gave her matching looks of outrage. The wails stopped though.

She tried to get control of herself, but the giggles kept coming.

"Why is Mama laughing? I was crying." Oh, Helena sounded so offended by that turn of events.

"I do not know why she is laughing any more than I know why you were crying," the great Alexandros Kristalakis admitted in a driven tone.

CHAPTER FOUR

HELENA'S FACE CRUMPLED, but she didn't start crying again. "Why you here, Papa?"

"Because he wants to be," Polly forced out between her inappropriate but cleansing humor.

The tension that had been building throughout lunch—and she wasn't even sure why—was gone.

"You sound very sure." The sarcasm was thick in her husband's tone.

But Polly just shrugged, finally getting her laughter under control and returning to her seat. If she didn't sound too confident it was because she herself had no clue why her husband was there for lunch for the second day in a row, with the unprecedented promise to work from home for the rest of the day, when he had never come home early in five years of marriage.

Alexandros frowned at Polly, but assured their daughter. "Yes. I want to be."

"Is Mama sick?" Helena asked her father fearfully.

"No, remember, I explained, honey? Mommy is just making your baby brother in her tummy. I'm not sick."

"But Papa is here."

"Yes." Polly didn't know what that had to do with her being sick.

"Lunch is for Mama and dinner is for Papa."

Polly tilted her head to the side. "But, Helena, your father is here during lunch on the weekends. Sometimes."

Alexandros winced at the *sometimes*. "I will be here more. I miss you and your mama, *koritsi mou*."

That was news to Polly. And she wasn't sure she believed it.

Their daughter looked no more convinced. "Faire's mama got sick and her papa had to take care of her."

"Who is Faire?" Alexandros asked, in what she thought was focus on the wrong thing entirely.

"One of your daughter's friends from playgroup," Polly answered before meeting her daughter's shimmering eyes. "I'm not sick, sweetheart. I promise."

"But Papa is here during the day. He's not here for the daytimes. He comes for bedtime. You are here during the daytimes. I don't want you to go away, Mama!" her daughter wailed, and then burst into tears all over again.

Alexandros placed Helena on Polly's diminished six-months-pregnant lap and then dropped to his knees so he could put his arms around them both. "No one is going anywhere. Mama is not sick," he said, adding his promises to Polly's, assuring their daughter that everything was all right and he was never going to let anything happen to her mama.

It took a while, but they got Helena settled down for her nap. In bed between Polly and Alexandros. It was not the first time they'd shared a family cuddle, but those times were rare. Polly couldn't even miss the intimacy she and Alexandros had been planning, because the moment was so special.

Besides, she needed her rest too and didn't fight her

eyes closing. "Wake me in time for the doctor appointments," she instructed her husband, who was no doubt going to take off and start working as soon as she fell asleep.

Only he was lying beside her when she woke, their daughter still asleep between them.

Feeling more refreshed than she had upon waking that morning, Polly smiled at him. "You're still here."

"The fact that my being in the vicinity is such a shock for both you and our daughter does not speak well of my presence in either of your lives."

Polly had no experience with her husband in self-examination mode. She wanted to comfort him, but his words were no less than the truth.

"No denials?" he asked, his expression troubled.

"Your business and family have always come first."

"You two are my family."

"Of course, but—"

"There is no but. You and Helena are the only family I could not live without. Don't you know that?"

"Um, no, not really." And just because he said the words didn't make them true. Even if he believed them, because his actions had said otherwise. Over and over again.

"And you do not believe me now," he said, showing that he was still in that disturbingly insightful mood.

"Not really, no." There was no point lying. He'd know, and besides, dishonesty wasn't her style. Except when she told him she was fine when she wasn't, and she had her reasons—maybe even conditioning—for doing that.

"Watch this space." With that, he climbed off the

bed coming around to help her up. "Come on, *agape mou*. Time for your appointments, chiropractic first."

More surprises awaited her as he insisted on attending both appointments with her, asking first the chiropractor and then the acupuncturist if there were things they could do to help her with the pain and nausea. Both doctors suggested weekly visits along with herbs and naturopathic solutions that would not impact her pregnancy negatively.

Alexandros only left when the acupuncturist explained that her treatment would be most efficacious if Polly spent time in peaceful contemplation with the acupuncture needles in place. She'd been shocked she had not even felt them going in and that they caused no discomfort at all as she lay, comfortably supported by pillows on the massage therapy table.

Soft piano music played in the background, the herbs the acupuncturist had used to further stimulate the flow of her energy giving off a soothing scent.

An hour later, Polly sat in a lounger by the pool, sipping water and watching her husband encourage their daughter to work on her swimming technique. Pain and nausea free for the first time in weeks, Polly didn't want to move and risk that happy condition.

So, when her daughter asked Polly to join them, she grimaced but went to stand anyway.

However, Alexandros waved her back onto the lounger. "Relax, *agape mou*. You can swim with us another day. The doctor said you needed to drink your water."

"All right." She relaxed back, wondering *if* there would be another day, as she took another sip of water under his watchful gaze.

Even on the weekends, time together as a family in the pool didn't usually happen. That was something that she and Helena shared during the day, during the week. Like so many things.

That weekend, they hosted their first family luncheon. Petros and Corrina arrived with Athena and Stacia in the helicopter but reached the house ahead of the two women.

"You look lovely and fresh today, Polly," Petros complimented after giving her a buss on both cheeks. "Where is my niece?"

"I put her down for an early nap, so she would be at her best when your mother and sister arrive." Polly turned to Corrina and hugged her. "I think married life is agreeing with you. You look wonderful."

Corrina was dressed in casual summer elegance, but it was the happy glow about the Greek heiress who had gone to school in England that brought a smile to Polly's own features.

"And you don't look nearly so tired as the last time I saw you. How are you feeling?"

"Really well. I've had a second session with the chiropractor, and both he and the acupuncturist are coming back in a couple of days."

Corrina grinned. "I'm still gobsmacked that Alexandros arranged all that."

"Would my brother not do whatever was in his power to make sure you were as comfortable as possible if you were pregnant with his child?" Alexandros asked chidingly, showing he'd been listening even if it had looked like he was busy greeting his brother.

Corrina blushed, giving Polly a *caught* look. She

smiled charmingly up at Alexandros. "Of course, but holistic medicine? Really?"

"It's been working for people for millennia."

"Well, of course..." Corrina let her voice trail off, clearly not sure what to say.

"It's working for me now." Polly laid her hand on Alexandros's arm. "I feel better than I have since getting pregnant."

He stilled and then slid his own arm around her waist in a jerky movement that was unlike his usual graceful self, pulling her so close, her entire side pressed into him.

She gasped, impacted by the touch far more than she should be. Pregnancy hormones.

As if he knew she was feeling things she shouldn't be in company, he turned her to face him and slashed a knowing smile down at her. "Feeling all right, *pethi mou*?"

Swallowing, she nodded.

He leaned his head down as if he was going to kiss her. In front of his brother!

But he frowned instead when his mother's voice came from the doorway to the drawing room.

"Stop pawing your wife in that common manner, and come greet your mother, Alexandros," Athena demanded imperiously. "I was surprised no one was outside waiting to greet our arrival."

The animation drained right out of his wife and she shifted, as if trying to step away from Alexandros.

But he had no intention of letting her go. "Not just yet," he said to her.

"What? But…" Pollyanna stared up at him, like he'd grown two heads. "Your mother wants you."

"And I want a kiss." He didn't wait for his wife to answer, but lowered his head and claimed her mouth.

With purpose. He wanted the life back, and in this, she always gave him spark.

For the count of three full seconds, Pollyanna did not respond at all, but then she relaxed against him and returned his kiss.

"Really, Alexandros, kissing your pregnant wife in company."

Pollyanna went stiff at his sister's snide tone, and Alexandros allowed her to step back when she pressed against his chest, pulling her head away from his. Ignoring both his mother and his sister for the moment, he cupped Pollyanna's cheek. "I find you irresistible, *agape mou*, but I'll keep. Did you want to go get Helena?"

Pollyanna nodded, her expression a cross between confusion and wary happiness.

He turned to face his sister and spoke before Pollyanna had a chance to leave the room. "I will kiss my *beautiful* wife where I like and in whatever company I find myself. Acting like a jealous cat because you don't have someone interested in doing the same with you only makes you look petty."

He flicked a glance over his shoulder and noticed that Pollyanna had a spring in her step as she crossed the drawing room that was rarely there in his mother and/or sister's company.

"How can you say something like that to me?" Stacia demanded, wounded eyes filling with tears.

Five years ago? He would have fallen for it and jumped in to apologize and promise she was still his number one girl. They'd both been grieving the loss of their dear papa, and he'd felt his new role as head of the family keenly.

Alexandros had grown older and hopefully wiser. He now realized that playing into his baby sister's need to be center of attention had done damage to his marriage and the way his wife perceived him. And he didn't think he'd done Stacia any favors either.

"I can say it because it is true. Keep a civil tongue in your head when you are here or you won't be invited back."

"You don't mean that," Stacia yelped. "You wouldn't exclude me from the family."

"I should have excluded you from socializing with my wife a long time ago." And how he was only realizing that in this moment did not speak well of his intelligence. "You are on notice. Take heed, or you will find more than just your social life curtailed in relation to me."

"What are you saying?" Stacia asked, her voice pitching.

"That you are old enough to find a job, if not a career, and your allowance is now on the bubble. A bubble that will burst if your behavior does not remarkably improve."

"I do not know what that wife of yours has been saying to you, Alexandros," his mother butted in. "But Stacia is your sister and calling her a jealous cat for being uncomfortable with an inappropriate public display of affection is not what I expect from you."

"There is nothing inappropriate about kissing my wife," he told his mother curtly. "And I stand by my warning." He gave Stacia a look. "Heed it."

His mother's mouth pursed with disapproval. "Your father left you head of the family and your sister is your responsibility."

For once, he didn't overlay the expression on her face with his own fear of her emotional fragility and saw his mother's attitude for what it was. Damaging to his wife.

And that would no longer be tolerated.

His mother had grieved the loss of his father, but just like all of them, she'd grown stronger and more able to deal with her pain.

Now was the time to let her know she didn't get to visit her disappointment that he had not married a Greek socialite on his wife. Ever again.

"One. Let's be clear. My wife hasn't said anything. Two. My sister is an adult, not a child. Three. If you want to take care of her monetary extravagances out of your own income, no one is stopping you."

"How dare you talk to me like this? You still have not even bothered greeting me. I raised you with more manners."

He walked forward and kissed both his mother's cheeks, then stepped back. *"Kalimera."*

"That is better."

He looked down at her, letting her see his expression was not a happy one. "Good. Now, make sure your daughter stays polite and we will all be happy."

Helena came running into the room, making a bee-line for Petros. "Uncle Petros, Uncle Petros!"

His brother swung the toddler up and asked how her nap was.

Helena shrugged, the movement so like something he would do that, not for the first time, Alexandros thought his wife had her hands full raising a child so like *him*.

"I slept," Helena informed her uncle.

"Would you like to say hello to your *yia-yia*?"

Helena tightened her hold on Petros, but nodded. Her usual vibrancy dimmed some, just as his wife's did, as his daughter looked at the older woman.

Why? He'd watched Helena interact with his mother. She was not afraid of her *yia-yia*, but she also wasn't enamored of her. And this was not normal for a Greek grandmother and her granddaughter, especially not his family. Alexandros could remember himself, his brother and their sister adoring their grandparents.

Helena should be thrilled to see her doting *yia-yia*.

Was it possible that Helena's relationship with her *yia-yia* had been impacted by his mother's less than approving attitude toward the little girl's beloved mom?

His daughter gave her grandmother a kiss of greeting on each cheek, accepting the same in return, but made no move to leave her favored uncle's arms to offer any further affectionate overtures. And Petros did not offer the child over either.

Neither did his mother reach for Helena.

In the past, he would have explained this response as a result of his wife's attitude toward his mother, and as such would have had a talk with his wife, expecting her to *fix* it. But recent insights had made him less quick to jump to that as the solution.

He would watch the way his mother, and his sister, interacted with his daughter.

And over the course of the next hours, he noticed things he had never noticed before.

Not only in the way his mother and sister related to his daughter, but in the very established patterns of their behavior toward his wife.

Even after the very serious warning he'd given his sister, she poked at Pollyanna, though admittedly without ever crossing the line to actual rudeness. Many of her comments had more than one meaning so she could claim easy deniability in the intent to offend.

"I don't understand why we couldn't keep dinners as they were. It's tradition. If Anna isn't up to joining us, surely you could have come on your own," Stacia said to him as they all relaxed on the terrace with after-luncheon drinks.

Pollyanna, though dressed as elegantly for lunch as the other women, played on the lawn with their daughter, Petros and Corrina joining them for a game of croquet that Alexandros realized he regretted not being a part of.

Every time it was Helena's turn to swing the mallet nearly as tall as she was, Petros stepped in to help her. On Helena's first turn, Pollyanna had moved as if to help, but Petros had said something and done so. No doubt realizing a pregnant woman didn't need to be bending over a toddler trying to navigate the mallet swing.

And Alexandros realized he wanted to be there, his arms around his daughter, playing with his family.

"She is my wife, which makes Pollyanna part of this family. Excluding her from family dinners because of her pregnancy, of all things, seems to defeat the purpose, don't you think?" They were Greek. They were Kristalakis. Family was paramount.

How did his sister think it was even acceptable to ask such a question?

His father would turn in his grave if he knew the attitude Stacia had toward the mother of the family's first grandchild of this generation.

"Your father started the tradition of family dinners on Sunday when I expressed a desire to have a set time for our family to be together, no matter what business the week might include," his mother said wistfully. "It is not so easy to give up something that makes me feel like he is still with us."

A week ago, Alexandros would have given in immediately to the subtle guilt trip, but he was on a rescue bid for *his* marriage and his parents' traditions could not supersede what was best for him and his wife.

Stacia and his mother wore twin expressions of expectation as they looked at him. Like they had no doubt his mother's words would change his mind about the new order of things.

"You and the rest of the family are still welcome to have your Sunday evening dinners, but I am a married man with a child and I should have stopped attending when Helena was born. Naturally, my wife and child should come first for me, should always have come first."

"You and your wife do not need to live in each other's pockets," his mother chided gently.

"Is that what you told my father? Only I remember you being very adamant that he spend those Sunday evenings with us, even if he was too busy the rest of the week."

His mother said nothing, her expression startled. Like she hadn't expected him to argue.

"Or are you implying that my wife and my daughter should be less important to me than you and our family were to my father?" he asked, beginning to realize the answer to that question was not always what he had assumed it was.

Alexandros had always believed that his mother respected his marriage and role as a father because of the expectations she had placed on his own father. Because family was *everything*.

But then, had he treated his wife and daughter like they were everything to him?

He wasn't sure he wanted to acknowledge the true answer to that question either.

"Of course I am not implying that," his mother said, but with a lack of conviction even Alexandros at his most blind could not have missed.

"Why didn't you ever suggest a change to our family dinners so you could see your granddaughter on a weekly basis?" he asked his mother.

"I already told you, I found our Sunday dinners a sentimental gathering I did not want to do without."

"Not even if it meant seeing your only grandchild?"

"Your wife could have arranged to bring the baby to visit," Stacia said with clear criticism.

"Surely it would have been easier for you to visit here," Alexandros said to his mother. "You were the one who suggested I move my pregnant wife out of the busy crowds of Athens."

He'd agreed because he'd thought that moving his wife out of the family home would circumvent the tension that existed between his mother and his wife.

Pollyanna had not reacted as he'd expected her to, accusing him of wanting to exile her to the country, of isolating her from the friends she'd managed to make despite the best efforts of his mother and sister in undermining her place in Athens society.

He'd dismissed the arguments as the result of pregnancy hormones and made it clear he would not tolerate her ongoing, and unnecessary, jealousy of his mother and sister.

Pollyanna was his wife.

There had been no need for her to be jealous of his family.

Or so he had believed.

"I still expected your wife to make the effort to share her daughter with us."

"Which she does." Once a month Pollyanna took Helena on the two-hour car ride to have tea with her grandmother. Alexandros did his best to join them when his schedule permitted.

Which admittedly wasn't as often as he now realized it should have been.

"So, why did we have to change family dinners?" Stacia asked, whining in a way that had been annoying when she was a teen and in adult woman was entirely unpleasant.

"We changed family dinners because if you want to share the time with me *and* my family, you will do so here and during the afternoon," Alexandros said implacably.

Neither his mother, nor his sister looked pleased by that response.

Had they always been this difficult?

Or had his policy of giving in to them to keep the peace blinded him to how intransigent and selfish both women could be?

Deciding he'd spent enough time discussing a situation that was not going to change, he stood up and excused himself so he could join the croquet players.

Swooping in to scoop his daughter up, he swung her up in the air, loving her joy-filled laughter.

Polly smiled at the way her daughter responded to attention from her father.

Helena adored her papa and Alexandros was a very hands-on dad when he was around. She was really glad to see that having his mother and sister here for lunch did not mean he would ignore his daughter for them.

Weekends were the only time Helena really got to play with her beloved papa, and Polly would have hated to see some of those hours lost because of the change to the Kristalakis once a week family gathering.

On Helena's next turn it was Alexandros who knelt beside his daughter, coaching her on the use of the mallet to tap the ball.

"I see how it is," Petros teased. "You saw Helena was winning and decided to horn in on the spoils of her victory."

"We are an unbeatable team, aren't we *koritsi mou*?" Alexandros asked his daughter.

Helena grinned up at her papa and then her uncle. "We're going to beat you, Uncle Petros."

Polly grinned at her daughter's arrogance, so like her father's. If anyone wondered how she still loved her husband after five years of marriage that had opened her eyes to how unimportant she was to him, all they had to do was look at Helena. How could Polly not love the man who had given her such a beautiful daughter?

More viscerally, how could Polly not love the man who was so like the child that she adored with every fiber of her being?

She saw the best of her husband in her daughter every day.

"Oh-ho, I see how it is. Now that your papa is here to play on your team, Uncle Petros is chopped liver."

Helena's tiny little face screwed up in disgust. "I do not like liver, Uncle Petros." She shivered dramatically and adorably, and looked up at Corrina. "It's yucky."

Corrina laughed. "You're right about that, Helena."

"Liver is good for you." His mother's voice from just behind Polly told her that the wicked witches of the west had joined them on the lawn.

Polly moved so she was on the other side of Petros without even thinking before she did it. When she could, she avoided even proximity with her mother or sister-in-law.

Alexandros whispered something into his daughter's ear that made Helena laugh and then they took their turn, neither one responding to his mother's quelling pronouncement.

"I hope you do not allow your daughter to dictate the food served her because she finds it *yucky*," Athena said to Polly with that superior tone she liked to take. "A child cannot be allowed to determine what is best for her."

"My daughter's diet is balanced and varied," Polly replied mildly.

"It was not as if *you* had anything to say about what we ate as children, Mama. That was entirely the nanny's purview."

Had those words come from Petros, Polly would only have been slightly surprised, but the fact her husband had made the comment that could be taken as standing up for *her* was downright shocking.

Her mother-in-law looked every bit as astonished as Polly felt. "Alexandros, naturally, your nanny acted on my instruction."

"If you say so, but no one of any intelligence would question the care my wife takes of our daughter. She is an exemplary mother in every aspect of that role."

Warmth burgeoned in Polly's chest, pleasure at that unequivocal vote of confidence from her husband filling her to bursting.

"I'm sure I wasn't questioning her mothering skills," Athena said repressively.

"I don't want to play anymore," Helena said from the circle of her father's arms.

"Why not?" he asked her.

"It's not fun now."

Out of the mouths of babes. Athena joined them and sucked the fun right out of the game, but Polly honestly didn't think her mother-in-law meant to do it. She was just so used to taking digs at Polly, she didn't realize the damage she was doing to her relationship with her granddaughter.

Polly had seen how Athena wanted to have a warmer relationship with Helena, but seemed incapable of understanding how to make that happen.

"Why don't we get out your Match the Cards game? Your *yia-yia* likes to play that with you," Polly suggested to her daughter. Then she turned a conciliatory smile on her husband. "She's probably getting tired."

But Alexandros frowned at his mother. "I do not think that is the problem."

Athena's expression showed vulnerable confusion, and Polly couldn't help feeling sorry for the older woman. So many of her machinations had led to final outcomes that were not to the widow's liking.

A doted-on heiress and then spoiled wife, Athena was used to getting what she wanted from the people in her life.

It had taken a while for both Polly and Athena to realize that Athena's attempt at excluding Polly from her social circle had backfired on her.

Polly had sought friendship with like-minded people, building the only kind of relationships she knew how. Real and based on shared ideas and attitudes. Those types of relationships engendered loyalty, both from her and the people she shared them with.

So, when Polly avoided social situations that would put her in proximity to Alexandros's mother or sister, her new friends noticed. And they stopped inviting those two women to whatever the event was if they wanted Polly to come.

She didn't join committees or charities which Athena or Stacia were attached to, and the same happened.

Athena had once accused her of doing it on purpose, but Polly hadn't. She wasn't petty.

No matter how her mother-in-law or sister-in-law had treated her, she had not set out to exclude them. However, by avoiding as many occasions as possible where she had to deal with being sniped at and undermined, it had happened inevitably. And honestly? It had made her life more pleasant.

But it had not been on purpose.

No more than this cooler relationship between her daughter and her *yia-yia* had been. Polly wanted Athena to enjoy the same pleasure of time spent with Helena as Polly's mom did.

But despite the fact that Polly's family only saw Helena a few times a year, the toddler adored them in a way she did *not* her *yia-yia* and Theia Stacia.

Because children might not understand the why, but they still picked up on the tension between the adults around them.

Polly was Helena's person. She was the one grown-up that Helena had trusted since infancy to always be there, to soothe, to play, to care for her.

Over time the fact that Athena made no effort to hide her disdain for her daughter-in-law in her grand-daughter's presence, that attitude eventually affected the amount of trust Helena gave Athena and how much pleasure she found in her *yia-yia*'s company.

Still, Polly did what she could to facilitate the relationship because ultimately, her daughter deserved it.

Polly put her hand to her lower back, rubbing a little. "I'm tired, even if our daughter isn't. I wouldn't mind watching you all play." Though she felt much better since her chiropractic appointment, playing croquet had maybe not been her best choice.

She did not expect what happened next. How could she?

But Alexandros passed their daughter over to Petros and then swept Polly up into his arms. "Of course you are tired. What were you doing playing croquet in your condition?"

Avoiding his mother and his sister.

"I'm pregnant, not an invalid," she said as millennia of women no doubt had been saying before her to their macho, overprotective spouses.

Not that she would have ever described Alexandros

as overprotective before, but apparently this pregnancy was bringing out his more basic nature.

"Papa is carrying Mommy," her daughter pronounced in shocked delight and then let loose a peal of laughter.

Polly found herself smiling at her daughter's clear amusement and noticed that Alexandros was smiling as well. He looked down at her, and their gazes caught, his smile turning sensual, hers growing intimate.

"Watch where you are going, brother, or you are going to trip and drop your pregnant wife." Petros's voice was laced with overt amusement.

Alexandros stopped, giving Polly a heart-stopping look. "He is right, but I find looking away from you a challenge."

"I could always walk on my own," she teased, when she had not felt like teasing him in a very long time.

His arms tightened around her. "No chance."

"You've grown very protective all of a sudden," she said just a little breathlessly.

"I have always wanted to protect you."

She winced and looked away. What was she supposed to say to that? He'd done a rotten job practically from the beginning, and for a man who prided himself on always getting it right, that had always said something to her. Something very negative about any chance that the man she married had really loved her and not just her body.

He cursed under his breath. A really basic word he *never* said in her presence much less his mother's.

Polly's gaze flew back to her husband's face.

"I failed utterly. That is becoming clear to me."

She shrugged. He had.

"Keep watching this space, *agape mou*. Failure is *not* in my nature."

CHAPTER FIVE

No. And being compared unfavorably to his younger brother in the husband stakes was not something Alexandros would take lying down.

Polly wasn't going to complain. Even if his reasons weren't the ones she wanted, her husband was finally treating her like she was important, and that was something she'd always wanted.

She'd built a life since her marriage without the need to have that desire filled, but it had always been there.

He carried her onto the terrace and settled her on a lounge chair, bringing her a glass of juice before sitting down at the nearby table to play the matching card game with his daughter, his mother, Petros and Corrina.

Uninterested in the child's entertainment, Stacia went inside with a comment about how hard her phone was to read outside.

Why her sister-in-law needed to be on her phone during what was supposed to be Kristalakis family time, Polly did not know, but she did not mind at all that the young woman wasn't expecting Polly to entertain her.

Polly found herself dozing, the sound of her daughter's and husband's voices a pleasant buzz in the background of her mind.

She surfaced from her doze to a conversation between her mother-in-law and husband.

"It is obvious she needs more rest than she is getting," Athena said with a concern Polly could not help doubting.

What was her mother-in-law up to?

"I think Anna is rather frail physically," Athena added.

Polly frowned. She was not frail, never had been.

"She is fine. A nap does not indicate frailty," her husband assured his mother.

"I do not know. Perhaps, and this is not something I like to talk about, but you should make sure she is getting a *full* night's rest rather than keeping her up."

Polly woke fully then, so furious she could barely breathe.

Her mother-in-law was trying to drive a wedge between Polly and Alexandros in the one area of their marriage that Polly felt confident of his full attention. The bedroom.

Polly sat up and turned so her feet were on the tile and she was facing to the two people standing near her. "Where is Helena?"

"Petros and Corrina took her inside. She wanted to watch one of her movies."

Polly knew exactly which one. Helena found the animated story about the Scottish princess who fought for the right to make her own choices obsessively fascinating. Honestly, Polly loved the movie too and didn't care that it wasn't one of the most recent children's offerings.

However, right now she wasn't thinking about princesses. She had her own wicked witch to deal with.

"Alexandros?"

"Yes, *yineka mou*?" He put his hand out to help her up.

She let him lift her, though standing in her flat sandals did not put her anywhere near eye to eye with her six-foot-four-inch husband.

Tilting her head back, she gave him a gimlet stare. "I know that there have been many times you've taken your mother's opinion of what *I* need over mine."

He inclined his head, his handsome mouth firming into a line.

"If you do that in this instance, I will not be responsible for my actions," she warned him.

"This instance?" he asked, while his mother gasped in clear outrage.

"The sex thing. You will not stop having sex with me on her say-so. Do you understand me?" Even her doctor had offered that as long as it was comfortable for Polly, sex was fine.

His eyes widened in obvious shock that she would approach the topic so bluntly.

His mother was saying something about not needing to talk about something that intimate in mixed company.

Polly glared at her mother-in-law, for once doing nothing to hide her anger with the older woman. "Then perhaps you should not have brought it up to my husband. Something that is so very much not *any* of your business."

"I was only trying to look out for your well-being," Athena claimed.

"No, you were trying to drive another wedge between your son and his wife, and I warn you, I have tolerated your interference for the last time in my marriage." Where the words came from, Polly didn't know.

But she meant them. And the look she gave her husband said it wasn't just his warnings that people had better take heed to.

Yes, she'd stopped and eavesdropped outside the drawing room while texting Hero to please bring Helena downstairs.

Athena did a very good impression of a woman mortally offended. "How can you speak to me like that?"

That was a good question. When was the last time Polly had even tried to stand up to the mother-in-law from hell? Before they'd moved to this house, before the birth of her daughter. Once Polly had realized just how little positive motivation lay behind Athena's machinations and how incredibly blind to that truth Alexandros was, Polly had shifted to oblique maneuvers to avoid rather than confront what she saw as something that could not be changed.

So why confront now?

Was it that *watch this space* from her husband that had felt so much like a promise?

Or was it simply that Polly was fed up?

"I have said what I needed to say to both of you." Polly encompassed both her husband and her mother-in-law with a look that Helena could have told them meant Mommy wasn't joking around here.

Then Polly turned to go inside and find the rest of their guests.

Stacia was pacing restlessly outside the drawing room from which the sounds of the movie could be heard. "Oh, Polly, there you are. Is my mother ready to go?"

"I do not know."

"Well, I am. This coming to the country once a week

is so inconvenient. I do not know why you had to go and convince Alexandros to change *our* family's traditional weekly get-together." Stacia gave Polly a less than pleasant look.

Polly just shook her head. "Alexandros already told you. The change was his idea, but you know something, Stacia? I'm just wondering, when are you going to stop sniping at me? Your brother and I are married, we are staying married and acting like a spiteful cat all the time isn't going to change that."

"He deserves better than you, and he only stayed married to you because of Helena."

"I didn't even get pregnant with Helena until after we'd been married a year. I don't know how you worked that one out."

"He was going to leave you. The move to this house was just the first step, but then you had Helena and he couldn't leave. A Greek man doesn't leave his children."

"An honorable Greek man does not leave his wife, or his children," Alexandros inserted into the conversation. "I have no idea where you got the idea that us moving to this house was in some way an indication I was finished with my marriage."

Polly met her mother-in-law's cool gaze. "I bet I can guess."

It was Alexandros's turn to shake his head. "This entire conversation is distasteful to me, and after my warning earlier I wonder, Stacia, how you thought you would get away with staging it."

"I don't think she can help herself," Polly offered. "Sniping at me has become so ingrained in her behavior, I don't think she knows how to react to me like an equal."

Alexandros made a sound of disgust. "That is not acceptable to me."

"You never cared before. I don't understand why you're acting like the fact your wife and I don't like each other matters to you now." Stacia's petulant attitude wasn't going to do her any favors with the man who was already angry.

Didn't his sister realize that?

He turned to Athena. "It is time you and Stacia left. Next week, do not bring her with you. She is no longer welcome in my home and I have paid the last installment of her allowance that she will receive from me."

"You can't do that!" Stacia screeched. "You're the head of this family. I am your responsibility."

"And if you ever manage to find someone willing to marry a shrew, I will pay for the wedding, but I'm done financially supporting a woman who treats my wife with such a lack of respect."

"I'll sue you!" she shouted.

"On what grounds?"

"Father left the company to you so you could take care of the rest of us."

"Father left each of us, including our mother, monetary assets as well as shares in the company. The fact that you ran through the lump sum you were awarded already is not my problem. The fact you cannot access your shares or the income from them until you are thirty is something you have to take up with your trustees."

"Of which you are one!"

"And not one who is going to argue for early dispersal," he said with freezing calm.

"Oh, for heaven's sake, Stacia, you are twenty-six

years old, you have a university degree. Get a job," Polly told her sister-in-law.

"Just because your family is happy to grub for a living, doesn't mean I'm going to stoop to doing so," Stacia seethed. She glared at her brother. "I will sue you. You just wait."

"You will not cause that kind of scandal, Stacia." Athena only despised one thing more than her daughter-in-law. Scandal. "Your brother gave you clear warning, and now you are paying the price for not listening. Perhaps if you apologized *politely* to Anna, Alexandros would see clear to continuing your allowance."

Polly bit her lip, because she had no doubt that an apology would not cut it.

Once Alexandros got to a certain point, he was immovable. Unfortunately for Stacia, she had not realized that he'd reached that place before he'd issued the warning before lunch.

"I'm very sorry if something I said might have offended you," Stacia said to Polly with one of the volte-faces Polly had grown accustomed to over the years.

Stacia could be in the middle of a spite-filled rant at Polly and turn up all smiles as soon as Alexandros was within hearing distance.

"You offended *me*," Alexandros made clear. "Your words were meant to *hurt* my wife and your apology is not accepted. It is time for you to leave."

Both Stacia and Athena objected then, but Alexandros would not be moved. Petros came out, closing the door to the drawing room behind him. "What is going on? You are making so much noise, I could hear you over the movie."

Polly went toward the door, needing to make sure

Helena wasn't upset by the altercation in the hall, but Petros put his hand up to stop her. "She's fine, totally enthralled by her warrior princess and singing along. How does she know *all* the words?"

"She's got her father's memory." And Helena had seen the movie multiple times.

With Polly. She could sing all the words too and would rather be doing that right now than arguing with Athena and Stacia. Not that Polly was arguing at all. She'd just been trying get calmer heads to prevail. No such luck though.

Alexandros was in pure head-of-the-family, my-word-is-law mode and his mother and sister, unused to him telling them no about anything were in screeching, this-can't-be-happening mode.

Athena and Stacia tripped all over each other to tell Petros what was happening, both women somehow managing to make it sound like Polly had started it all, when in fact she had started nothing. Alexandros took immediate exception to the implications and the argument raged again.

Polly looked longingly at the closed door.

At one point, Athena said, "If you ban Stacia from family lunches I will not feel I can come either."

"You will have to do as you think best," Alexandros replied without hesitation, shocking everyone, including Polly.

She stared at her husband, feeling like he'd been taken over by aliens. Since when did he do or say anything that would upset his mother? Okay, today. But it had been a first.

Not fulfill the family tradition of the weekly get-together? That was simply not possible.

"Alexandros—" Petros started, his tone conciliatory.

But Polly's furious husband cut in before his brother could say anything more. "What, Petros? Would you allow either of them to speak to, or about, your wife the way they've been with Pollyanna?"

Petros's mouth snapped shut and then he shook his head decisively. "No, I would not."

"Corrina is everything a wife should be," Stacia said with umbrage. "She's beautiful, has been educated at the best schools. She's Greek, from a good family and she has her own fortune."

"While I am none of those things and come from a middle-class American family," Polly said with no shame. Because she was not and never had been embarrassed about her upbringing.

Her parents were good people. Her siblings were amazing, and not one of them would ever treat someone the way Stacia and Athena had since the first day Polly had stepped foot in Greece.

Polly had been all set to be the best daughter-in-law she could. She'd had all the sympathy in the world for a woman who had lost so many important people in her own life in too few years, but Athena had not wanted an American upstart as part of her family. And she'd made sure Polly knew it.

Stacia's jealousy and spite had only added to Polly's discomfort.

"You are beautiful. You are educated," Alexandros said to her now. "You are American, but have adapted amazingly well to living in my home country and I don't need you to have a fortune to know that mine has never been much of a draw to you."

Polly's eyes filled with tears. Darn pregnancy hormones. "I just wanted you."

"And I only wanted you. I don't need a wife with a pedigree. I need *you*."

She'd always had something that outstripped a pedigree for him. Her body. He could not resist her and the feeling was mutual. It might not be the love she'd believed she'd had when she got married, but it wasn't anything to dismiss either. The kind of passion they shared was rare and very precious.

Both her sisters were deeply in love with their husbands and loved in return, but both had shared with Polly that their sex lives were adequate. While hers? Was spectacular. And she didn't dismiss that as nothing of importance.

"I need you too," she said in a wobbly voice.

He jerked his head, like her words had touched a live wire inside him. Then he pulled Polly into his arms and against his chest. "Petros, please escort Mama and Stacia out to the helicopter."

Simply ignoring his mother's and sister's continued protests, Alexandros guided Polly into the drawing room, settling them both on the sofa with their daughter and even contriving to sing along to some of the songs with Polly and Helena.

As if the big argument had not happened.

Polly paused just inside the drawing room. "You might consider giving them a break."

"What?" He stared down at her like she was the one who was acting out of character.

"Your mom and sister are used to getting their way. Maybe give them a chance to adjust to the new family normal before you ban them from family lunch and stop giving your sister an allowance."

"You told her to get a job," he reminded her.

"Honestly? It would do her good, but I think you could ease into it. Give her a month to find something she's willing to lower herself to do. You know?"

"I'll think about it."

"And your mom?"

"Made her own choice about not coming for the family luncheon."

Polly couldn't deny that. "But if she changes her mind?"

"I will welcome her to my home as always."

Petros and Corrina stayed the night, flying back into Athens with Alexandros the next morning.

Polly found her more relaxed schedule a lot more pleasant than she'd expected it to be, and she loved having as much time as she wanted to play with Helena.

When her daughter went down for her nap after lunch, Polly relaxed with a book. She didn't remember the last time she'd been able to read just because she wanted to.

Curled up in her favorite lounge chair in her room, she was surprised when the door opened.

Beryl was attending a meeting on Polly's behest and Dora had already left for the day. Of course, any one of the other servants could have decided they needed to talk to Polly about something, but she was rarely interrupted when she was in her sanctuary.

She looked up, waiting to see who needed her and was startled at the sight of her husband.

"I didn't hear the helicopter." Had he told her he was coming home early?

She didn't remember him doing so.

He looked at the book in her hand. "When you are lost in a book, a bomb could go off and I am not sure you would notice."

"I haven't gotten to really enjoy a good read in so long, I guess I forgot." She cast a quick glance at the baby monitor, relieved to see the lights indicated her daughter was still sleeping. "I'll have to rethink reading while Helena is napping if I didn't hear the helicopter."

"I'm sure our daughter's voice would penetrate. Your mother instincts are too strong for it not to." Alexandros looked around the room like he'd never been in there before. Maybe he never had.

It was her sanctuary, but she never came to this room in the evenings when he was home.

"You've put your mark on this room."

"I redecorated it when I did the nursery."

"You never said."

"You never said I couldn't."

"Of course you could. This is your home. You could redecorate the entire villa if you wanted to."

She shrugged. "I spend my time in here and in the nursery. I don't need to redecorate anywhere else."

"That my wife, who spends more time here than anywhere else, restricts her living to a few hundred square feet of thousands does not speak well of your comfort in your home."

He was just now noticing? But she smiled. "I use the pool. And the dining room of course, and the breakfast nook." She preferred the smaller sunny room, even if the decor was just as generically modern as the rest.

"And the terrace. Helena and I spend a lot of time on the terrace." She'd had a play structure installed at one end for her daughter and her daughter's friends to use when she hosted the playgroup.

"I noticed you don't use the media room for watching movies with Helena."

"It's too much. We've used it to host a movie afternoon for her playgroup." The parents had been impressed, but the littles hadn't found the theater style seating as comfortable as piles of pillows on the floor of the still admittedly formal drawing room.

Instead of looking happier at her list of the places in the villa that Polly and Helena used, her husband's face took on a pained expression. "It's your home. You should feel comfortable *everywhere*."

"Childproofing rooms that were decorated with a then childless billionaire in mind hardly seems worth it when Helena and I are perfectly content to use the areas best suited to her needs."

"I never considered the childproofing aspect." He frowned. "You said it was decorated with me in mind, not you."

"Obviously." Polly would never have gone for all the marble and neutral shades. And knowing she was pregnant, though not having shared the news yet at the time with him, she would never have put so many expensive objets d'art on display where tiny fingers could reach them.

He winced. "It is your home," he reiterated. "It should reflect your taste."

"That is not what you said when we moved in." He'd been livid she hadn't appreciated his effort in hiring a popular interior design firm to do the entire house at great cost.

"Perhaps I've learned something in three years."

She shrugged. "It doesn't matter anymore." She'd gotten used to living in a mansion that felt like a high-end hotel.

"The existence of this room says otherwise."

"I wanted a place that felt like home."

"And the other ten thousand square feet of the villa?"

"Feels like one of Zephyr and Neo's hotels." The property developer duo didn't socialize as much as others in their position. Both were firm family men with lovely wives that had befriended Polly her first year in Greece.

The friendship had come as a double-edged sword. Polly loved spending time with the Stamos and Nikos families, but seeing the devoted husbands and fathers that both Zephyr and Neo made was hard when her own billionaire didn't seem to get how to manage that feat.

She couldn't just dismiss his neglect and business-oriented priorities as the necessary challenges of a man in his position when she saw others who handled their family lives differently.

Even now she clung to the consolation that Zephyr and Neo had a very different background from Alexandros, and neither had a snooty family to pacify.

Displeasure creased Alexandros's handsome features. "In other words, transitory."

She'd never thought of it that way, but maybe he was right. "Maybe."

"Our marriage is not temporary."

"Your mother and sister both wish otherwise," Polly acknowledged wryly.

It was something she would have not have said even before yesterday, but he had stood up for her in a way he never had and she felt some of the confidence she'd had early in their marriage returning.

The grim set of his lips said he got her point. "I should have set them straight about the way they treat you a long time ago."

"If you had, it's probable that the schism that happened yesterday wouldn't have." Polly might have understood some of Alexandros's attitude in the beginning of their marriage when his family was still mired in grief, but that didn't change the truth. "They both got used to saying whatever they wanted to, and about, me. Neither took you seriously when you warned Stacia to watch her tongue yesterday."

"But you did?" he asked.

She had, as shocking as she'd found his late in the game championship of his wife. "I know that look you get when you will not be moved, and you had it."

"And yet my mother and sister, who have known me since my birth and hers respectively, did not recognize this look?"

"Maybe they've never seen it before. Your usual policy with them is to give them what they want." He'd once told her he expected peace on the domestic front.

And he'd shown her that the way he ensured it was to give his mother what she wanted *like a good son*, and to spoil his sister because that was what everyone in that family expected of him toward Stacia.

"While depriving my wife of the support she should expect from me." He did not sound impressed by that concept.

She wasn't either, but she'd learned to live with it. "No comment."

"You used to tell me I spoiled them."

"You did." And he'd had his reasons, but yes, definitely spoiled.

"And yet, no matter how I provided for you materially, *you* never felt spoiled by me."

"I needed different things from you." Time. Attention. His willingness to stand by her side in a family confrontation.

"Needed past tense?" he asked.

"I learned to find contentment with what I had."

He said an ugly word, and suddenly she realized he was seethingly angry.

"You're furious," she said, feeling fragile and not even sure why.

"Ne."

Yes, she translated.

Polly bit her lip. "With me?"

Suddenly his face changed completely, and he pulled her into his arms without warning. "With myself. With my mother and my sister, who should have made you welcome, but instead did much to guarantee you found life here as my wife difficult. But mostly with myself, *agape mou*, mostly with myself."

He kissed her then, his lips gentle and completely at odds with the emotion pouring off of him.

She responded, as she always did, allowing her body to melt into his, parting her lips for the tender caress of his tongue. They kissed for long minutes, the only sound in the room their shared breathing and their daughter's sleeping snuffles over the monitor.

Finally, he pulled back and made a point of looking around her sanctuary. "I like it in here."

"I do too."

"I would like it if you brought this warmth into the rest of our home."

"Would you?" She didn't remind him again that he'd changed his tune.

Because the fact he had? Was something good.

"Not immediately and not all in one go." He brushed a barely there kiss across her lips. "I do not want you exhausted by another project when we've worked to take others off your plate."

"We?" she asked delicately.

"Okay, I made some unilateral decisions, but you looked relaxed and pink with health when I arrived. I do not think that can be seen as anything but a positive."

Believing positive reinforcement might work as well with the father as with the daughter, she gave him a warm, approving smile. "I have enjoyed my more re- laxed schedule."

"Do you *like* the charity work?" he asked for the first time ever.

"You mean my job as your wife?" Because that's what it was.

Once they'd gotten married and moved her into the family home, he had laid out a whole set of expecta- tions for how she was going to live her life that she had not anticipated.

"Is that how you see it?"

"What else? You even give performance reviews," she teased.

But it was true. Especially when they were first mar- ried, he'd make sure to take time to talk about what he felt she was getting right and what he thought she could improve on in her public role as his wife. Unfortunately, she'd discovered that public role took a lot more of her private time than she'd ever wanted it to.

In the beginning, she would have been happier if she could have gotten a job in her field, but his mother had thrown a fit at the idea of Polly working as a *menial laborer*, which is how she considered Polly's formerly demanding career as a pastry chef. Later, Polly would have preferred more uninterrupted time to dedicate to being Helena's mom.

"No, I do not think I have ever considered your role as my wife in the light of a job before." And his tone said he didn't like seeing it that way either. "As to what you call performance reviews, I was only trying to help you find your way in a very different world to the one you left behind."

"It never occurred to you that it would have been a lot easier to find my way if I had been allowed to maintain what I could from my life in America."

"What do you mean?"

"If I had been able to get a job as a pastry chef, I would have made friends more quickly and with workmates." She pulled away from him and walked over to look out the window. "I know those weren't the people you *wanted* me to make friends with, but I wasn't raised in your rarified atmosphere and it would have been a lot easier for me to have some friends who understood my middle-class outlook on life."

"I thought that in the long run you would settle in better if you made relationships in that 'rarified world' as you call it where you were now living."

She spun back to face him. "Then why dump me in

the back of beyond, taking me away from the friends I had managed to connect with?"

"I thought you would be happier in the country. You were raised in rural Upstate New York."

"With you gone during the week and living in this great honking hotel?" she asked with disbelief. "No wonder your mom and sister considered the move the beginning of the end of our marriage."

Only no one had counted on Polly turning up pregnant. It wasn't as if she and Alexandros had been trying for a baby. They'd agreed they wanted to wait at least two years before they started trying, and Polly had grave misgivings about having a baby with him by the end of the first year of their marriage.

But she'd gotten the flu and her pills had been rendered ineffective. Not that she, or he, had realized it. Not until she'd started losing her breakfast.

"I do not know where Stacia got the idea that my buying this house was an indication that I saw our marriage as anything but permanent."

Polly twisted her lips at how he ignored the truth of her comment as he had so often in the past. "Probably a combination of believing what she wanted to and the fact that for almost the first year after we moved here, you spent most of your work week in the Athens apartment and only came home on the weekends."

And those had been shortened from Saturday afternoon to before dawn on Monday morning, when he'd fly out again. Polly had no intention of glossing over the reality of what her marriage had been like then.

Even *she* had wondered if he had intended the move as a way to make her a smaller player in his life, if not a prelude to the dissolution of their marriage.

"I was fighting the takeover and then working like hell to make sure it could never happen again." Frustration laced his voice. "Everything my father and his father and grandfather before him had built was resting on my shoulders, but also the livelihood of tens of thousands of employees."

CHAPTER SIX

HE'D BEEN DOING the best he could for his family.

Polly could see now that was how Alexandros had seen it. And honestly? She could not dismiss all those employees and their lives as being unimportant. He'd hurt her, but he hadn't done it on purpose, and he hadn't ignored her just to make another few million.

Moving her to the back of beyond and acting like he was doing her a favor? That was something else. Something maybe they still needed to work out between them.

Because she had missed the country, and she'd told him so, but she hadn't expected that to result in being moved away from the friends she still missed, or the opportunities to cook in the soup kitchens that had offended her mother-in-law so much, or the easier access to *him*.

"But Stacia didn't know that." Neither had Polly, if it came right down to it. "She and your mother took your behavior to mean that you'd lost interest in our marriage. It's natural they came to the conclusion that you only stayed married to me because I was pregnant with Helena."

"But you know that is not true."

Polly didn't answer right away. Because she *had* believed that.

Just as she'd felt trapped in a marriage that was nothing like what she'd expected or wanted it to be, she'd assumed he was equally trapped by her pregnancy. If Polly ever had considered divorce in that first year, those thoughts were stopped cold by the discovery she carried his child.

She'd owed her daughter the best form of stability she could give her.

Polly had always believed Alexandros had felt the same.

He stared at her, like reading her thoughts on her face. Maybe he was. Even her own mother told Polly she wore her heart on her sleeve.

Unless she was channeling her Anna persona, but that crutch had been harder to lean on lately.

With a curse, Alexandros strode across the room and swept Polly into his arms. Then he sat down on the love seat where Polly liked to give Helena a cuddle while she read to her daughter. This time it was Polly sitting on Alexandros's hard thighs, his arms steel bands around her. Like he was afraid she'd disappear if he let go.

She dismissed the fanciful thought, and said, "I think me getting pregnant with Helena was a wake-up call for both of us."

She'd realized her marriage was something she had to make work. And he'd… Well, she thought he'd realized pretty much the same thing.

"My wake-up call came last weekend at my mother's home."

Polly gasped.

It was the first time he'd referred to the family villa

as being his mother's home and not his as well. Even after they'd moved to the country, he referred to the family villa as home.

She was so stunned that it took a few seconds for the rest of what he said to sink in. And she almost smiled. Almost. Because it hurt a little. That she'd been right. That believing he wasn't measuring up to his own brother as a husband had sparked the amazing transformation in Alexandros's viewpoint toward his marriage and Polly.

"Nothing to say?"

"Not a lot, no." She had realized she had to make their marriage work, even if it meant changing her own expectations, when she was pregnant the first time.

Regardless of whether or not his ego had prompted it, Alexandros had come to something of the same conclusion a week ago.

"Better late than never?" she tried.

He grimaced. "You consider your role of my wife as a *job*?" he asked, proving he was still stuck on that point.

"What would you call it when I have a list of duties to perform that have nothing to do with our personal relationship? When I have a set of expectations for how I must spend my days?" The bitterness in her own voice surprised her.

But he'd opened this Pandora's box in their marriage.

She'd shut the lid tight on her personal dreams and expectations when she realized that no matter how much she fought him, she *was* trapped in a marriage that wasn't anything like she'd thought it would be. That whatever else her husband felt for her, it wasn't love and that no matter what, their unborn child deserved a stable and content homelife.

"I…" He let his voice trail off, without a ready response.

If she could believe it. And she found that very difficult. He was never without a ready response.

"So, you *don't* like the charity work?" he asked finally.

"It's not that black-and-white."

"Isn't it?"

"Do you like spending time with me and Helena?"

"You know I do."

"So, sell off your company and spend all your time with us."

He stared at her in nothing less than abject horror. "You don't mean that."

"It's not that black-and-white, is it?"

He sighed. "I suppose not." For Alexandros?

That was quite the climbdown.

"When we talked about having children before we got married, do you remember what we said?" She looked into the espresso gaze that had so caught her that first time their eyes met and willed him to think back.

"That we both wanted you to be able to stay home with our children."

"And you promised me that I could. You said you understood that I wanted to be the mom who was home after school, that our house would be the one that our children and their friends hung out in. Even if it was a mansion." He'd used those exact words.

"You are an at-home mother." Confusion made his body tense against hers.

He had never liked not understanding. Anything.

"Am I?" Only she didn't feel like one when the charity work and social events he insisted she had to host and attend were as demanding as any full-time job. "Today I got to play as much as I wanted to with Helena. I got to help her make cookies for the first time without planning the event two weeks in advance on my calendar."

There had been a time that Polly spent time baking every day, just to relax. She'd clung to that in the first year of their marriage, but obligations on her time and her mother-in-law's attitude toward such pursuits eventually saw the end to her indulging in her passion for creating.

"In fact, it was one of the few times I've been in the kitchen with our daughter because there are so many things I want to do with her and there simply isn't enough time to do them. She spends a lot of her time with me, in here, while I work with Beryl, my attention divided."

"You do make it sound like a full-time job, but you must understand. This is how I was raised. I grew up with a mother who kept such social obligations as a matter of course." And a grandmother before that.

She knew it was ingrained in him to see life a certain way by his family, by his history, by his culture and by his own personal experience. That didn't make it any easier for Polly to live the life he expected of her.

"Your mother never held any other job, and she relies a lot more heavily on her personal staff than I ever had," Polly pointed out.

"Because you believe that if a job is worth doing, it is worth doing right."

"And personally." Polly wasn't putting her name to

something she wasn't actually personally involved in, but recently she'd begun to realize that maybe her own stubbornness had pushed her to a higher level of involvement than necessary.

That wasn't an easy thing to acknowledge or admit. Because it meant that not only was some of her discontent with her life at her own instigation, but her own pride and intransigence had led her to taking time away from Helena that she hadn't needed to.

"I know that a lot of moms don't have the time they want with their children," she acknowledged to him, for now not addressing her inner revelations. Not ready to share the burden of blame when *so* much rested on his attitudes and expectations. Still, she added, "I try very hard to remember that my life is easy in comparison to other women's."

"Because you are rich."

"Because my husband is a billionaire."

"What is mine is yours." He said it like he believed it.

But again she thought it was a matter of him believing something in the abstract, but his actions showing a deeper conviction toward something else.

"Not according to the prenup. And honestly? If that were true, you would not have bought this house without my input." Could he finally understand that had been taking his tendency toward control one giant step too far?

"That was a mistake."

Again, shock rendered her nearly mute, but she managed to force out, "Was it?"

"You are my wife." He cupped her cheek, his hand warm against her skin. "I should never have made the decision to move us out of Athens without your agreement."

Polly was kind of stunned he was admitting it finally. "I didn't want to live with your mother and sister any longer." Even though, at first, she'd been okay with it.

He'd explained how the villa had been their family home for generations. How his mother had begged them to make their home there rather than him moving out. In the light of Athena's recent losses, Polly's heart had been moved to agree.

And she'd moved into the villa, believing she could help heal the family's grief only to learn that nothing she said or did was going to endear her to Athena or Stacia.

"But when you bought Villa Liakada, I'd made friends in Athens, built a life for myself. You took it all away."

"And thought I was doing you a favor in the process," he said with a self-deprecating twist to his handsome lips.

"Yes."

"I hurt you."

Many times. "Yes."

He winced, his own expression revealing a vulnerability she wasn't sure she could believe. "I have always wanted you to be happy in our marriage."

"I've found contentment."

He leaned down, pressing his forehead to hers. "Damned by faint praise."

"It could be worse," she admitted, whispering because she felt like there was a fragile bubble of intimacy around them she did not want to break.

"I could be a philandering abuser," he said with pure self-derision she had never seen him point at himself.

"Believe it, or not, but I need to be something better in your life than that."

Suddenly that bubble was suffocating, and she couldn't stand being in his arms, held like something precious when so many times she had not mattered to him at all.

She pushed against him, but he resisted.

"Let me go, please." She needed to breathe.

He released her, his expression one she did not want to try to interpret right then.

She stood and moved to where her book sat on the table by the chair she'd been in earlier. Needing something to do, she slotted it back into the bookshelf. "I think we married too quickly, without really realizing what the other person wanted."

She didn't claim they were both too young, because Polly had been twenty-seven and Alexandros had been thirty-two.

They'd met when he was in the States. She'd done the desserts for a meeting he attended, and somehow the middle-class pastry chef had bumped into the billionaire.

That first meeting had been electric, and she hadn't even hesitated when he'd asked her to dine with him the following evening. She'd fallen for him hook, line and sinker. And she'd thought the tsunami of emotions had been two-sided.

Six weeks later, they were engaged and he was headed to Asia for more business talks. They saw almost nothing of each other in the three months leading up to the wedding, but she'd thought their phone calls, texts and emails had built a foundation she could rely on.

She met her mother-in-law at the wedding rehearsal.

Athena had been reserved, but not overtly hostile. She'd worn black, claiming she was still in mourning for her deceased husband. Since he had died only a little over a year previous, Polly had believed.

Since then, she'd had cause to wonder that color choice for the mother of the groom.

Their month-long honeymoon had been bliss, but then her real life as the wife of an old-money Greek billionaire began. And it had not been anything like a fairy tale.

Polly stood there, staring at the spines of the books she hadn't had time to read and wondered where they went from here?

Alexandros clearly wanted to improve their marriage.

She didn't know if she could trust him enough to open herself to trying.

"If you had it to do again, would you have married me?" he asked her, having come up behind her without her realizing.

He laid his hands on her shoulders, turning her around so their gazes met. His was filled with a nameless emotion. Hers, she knew, would be wary.

Because she felt wary.

She stifled a sigh. "That's a pointless question. We *did* get married. We did have a daughter. We do have a son on the way."

"I wasn't there to learn the sex of either of my children." It sounded like he really regretted that.

"I told you."

"*Ne*. You told me. The first time with a sweet little pink cupcake that tasted like ambrosia and stopped my heart with the knowledge you were carrying my daughter."

But for their son, she'd texted. We're having a boy. The joy-filled phone call had gone to her mother and the special cupcake? She'd made for Helena.

Her daughter had squealed and insisted on sitting down right then to draw a picture to put on her baby brother's nursery wall.

"I bought champagne for the entire office staff to celebrate that text," he said, proving their thoughts were running on similar tracks.

"And a pair of sapphire earrings for me," she said.

"No alcohol while you are pregnant."

"They're lovely earrings."

"But you would have been more touched if I'd bought a stuffie."

She shrugged. "Maybe, but I knew you wanted me to know you were happy about the baby. And that's what matters."

"I am happy about the baby. I adore Helena and cannot wait to welcome her little brother into the world."

"I'll be giving birth soon enough." In about fourteen weeks if all went to plan.

"I plan to be there for the entire labor and delivery this time," he told her.

"If you can't, I'll manage. Mom and Dad already have plans to be here a week before the due date, and they're both staying a full month this time."

"Nevertheless, I will be there."

Polly didn't reply. She didn't want to call him a liar, but she doubted even the certainty he would be in the country when she gave birth.

He sighed. "I think I've broken too many promises to you without ever meaning to."

"I think if it had been intentional I wouldn't have stayed, but even I could tell that we just didn't see the world the same way."

"There is no reason that Beryl cannot continue on as she is now, even after the baby is born."

Polly pushed back her knee-jerk reaction of denial and considered what she really wanted, and what would be best for her and the two children she would have. "I would like that."

"Then, that's the way it will be." He stepped back, and she contrarily missed his warmth.

She moved away from the bookcase, tidying up the few things that were not in their proper place. Hope was a terrifying ember burning in her heart. Polly could not snuff it out, but the fear that it would lead to more pain down the road wouldn't go away either.

He looked around her sanctuary again, a small smile playing on his lips. "I should have begged Zephyr Nikos to convince his wife to do the decor here in the villa. Despite you comparing this place to one of their hospitality properties, you and she share a similar design aesthetic."

Polly smiled. The thought of having Piper redecorate the villa was a pipe dream, but something she would have loved.

"Would you like to move back to Athens?" Alexandros asked with every evidence of being serious.

But could he really mean it?

Most of the friends she'd made in Greece still lived in Athens, or visited there. Corrina and Petros were there, and they were her very best friends. Helena adored them and would love to see her uncle and new aunt more often.

But Polly forced herself to think beyond what would make her happy. "I'm not sure it would be fair to Helena. She's never known any other home than this one. And she has friends in her playgroup."

"The constant in her life is you, Polly. Not this house." Alexandros gave her the slashing smile that had first caught her eye. "You are an amazing mama. She will make other friends. And if I know you, you'll make sure she still gets to visit her current playmates. After all, you are the woman who makes sure our daughter sees her *yia-yia* once a month despite how my mother has treated you."

"You are a constant for her too," Polly offered, because it was true. And because maybe it needed to be said. "You are a good father."

Maybe he wasn't around as much as her father had been for Polly, but Alexandros loved his daughter very much and it showed.

"I am glad you think so. Very glad, but the truth is, *both* of you see less of me than you should because of the daily helicopter commute."

"We *would* see more of you if we lived in Athens," she acknowledged.

Not only was there the daily commute to consider, but he spent at least one night a week in Athens, which cut their family time down even more.

"We'll take as many of our staff with us as are willing to move." He was talking like it was a done deal.

Even so, as much as she might like that, she didn't see their staff traveling to Athens with them. "A lot of them have family in the area."

"I'll offer a significant moving bonus and the two-hour drive is not so onerous they can't make it to visit family."

"You would do that, so that she has continuity of homelife?" Polly asked, a little shocked at the idea they could take the staff, many of whom had become friends, with them.

"I would do that so that *you* don't have to get used to new people either."

It was true that getting used to new staff when she'd moved in here after only just adjusting to the staff at the Kristalakis family home had been very hard for a woman who had grown up doing everything for herself. Her family came to visit more often now they'd gotten used to the staff too; she didn't want them to cut down their visits again either.

"Would we find the house together?" she asked, unwilling to make another major move without input in where they ended up.

"That is important to you, doing it together?"

"I don't want to live in another hotel."

"You could pick it out."

Disappointment filled her. "You're probably too busy to take time off to house hunt with me."

She went to turn away, but he grabbed her and gently pulled her into his body again. He'd always been a physical lover, but he was so much more touchy-feely right now.

And she kind of loved it.

Not that she was admitting that one out loud. It would make her sound needy.

"Not at all," he assured her.

She didn't know what he saw on her face, but he

cursed in Russian. A habit he'd developed after Helena's birth so he didn't accidentally say a word she might repeat in Greek or English.

Alexandros pressed their bodies close and groaned. "Our daughter is going to wake up any minute and Hero will not be on duty for hours yet."

Polly hid her grin at his impatience. "You'll survive."

"If you were living in my skin, you would not be so sure." Then he went all serious again. "I want you to be happy in our next home."

"So, give me the final right of choice," she challenged.

"Done."

She let the grin take over her face. "Watch out, you'll end up in a farmhouse."

"In Athens? I am not worried, *yineka mou*."

"So, we are really moving?" she asked, disbelief more prevalent than acceptance.

"Our primary residence, yes."

"You mean we're keeping the villa?" Relief she would not have expected washed over her, but this was the house she'd brought her baby home to.

The first house that had been only hers and Alexandros's.

"That is entirely up to you, Polly. This house is in your name." He kissed her lightly. "But if I get a vote, I would like to consider keeping it. I would still like to get out of the city on occasion and think it would be good for our children as well."

She could only nod. The house was *hers*? But according to the prenuptial agreement, anything he bought for her she got to keep in the eventuality of a divorce.

She'd never considered he might buy her a house that had cost several million euros.

"I think your brother and Corrina will be glad of that, too," she said for lack of anything better to say. Her mind was still melting under that knowledge that Polly owned the villa.

Alexandros's smile was warm. "You are very close to them."

"I am."

"I am glad."

Even after that closeness led to his being challenged in his perception as a husband? That was a pretty nice sentiment actually. Especially for a man as proud as her husband.

"I'm six months pregnant." It just popped out. She hadn't been thinking of her pregnancy as a stumbling block to moving, but the truth was this pregnancy had been really hard on Polly and she wasn't sure she was up to it.

"You think this is a bad time to make the move?" he asked, like that mattered more than anything else. "You know I won't allow you to do too much. We'll have movers and professional packers. You'll only have to supervise."

She didn't mention that supervision could be very taxing, simply looked at him and asked. "Will you help?"

"In every way that I can. I promise."

She nodded. Beryl would as well, even if they had to hire her a second assistant.

Polly discovered that house hunting with her billionaire husband was nothing like she might have expected.

He hired *the* preeminent estate agents in Athens who then provided virtual walk throughs on potential properties.

She'd pictured going to look at houses together, but so far, they had both watched the videos separately and then discussed them. Usually after tucking their daughter in for the night.

They were spending more time together however because her workaholic husband had come home early again this week, twice. And he had arranged to work from home once, without a single overnight at the Athens apartment.

Helena was blossoming under the extra attention from her beloved papa. Polly was blooming too, but fear of going back to the way things had been cast a shadow over her enjoyment of her husband's increased presence.

Polly was leaning back against Alexandros's chest as they looked at potential property together on his phone. It was one she'd gotten very excited about.

"If you are that keen on this house, you could go see it with the agent tomorrow," he told her.

She felt her body tense. "I thought we were visiting the properties together."

"I cannot do it tomorrow."

"What happened to no more uncomfortable helicopter rides into Athens for me?"

"I thought you and Helena could come to the apartment for the rest of the week, perhaps longer."

They would be right across the hall from Corrina and Petros. And Alexandros's office would be an elevator ride away. Excitement coursed through Polly. "You've never invited us to the penthouse."

He used one when he stayed over, while Corrina and Petros lived in the other full-time. One floor below were a set of four apartments used by the company for business related needs, but the penthouses were gorgeous from the pictures Corrina had sent Polly on her phone after moving in.

"I've had the penthouse childproofed and a plexiglass guard added to the balcony railing, which I've had raised another two feet. Not that you'll allow Helena out there without supervision, but it's an extra measure of security for her." Tossing away his phone, he tugged her into his lap, so their gazes met. "And I never realized you needed an invitation to join me in Athens."

"I didn't?" she asked, stunned by the concept that he would have welcomed her presence and that of their daughter at any time.

"No. I realize now that I had made it seem like to you that I saw you as separate from my business life, but I don't. Everything is for and about you and Helena and our unborn son now."

"But..."

"If you want the truth, it hurt that you never came to stay, especially those times I had to spend more than a night in the city." He frowned, swallowed, looked away and then back at her, like he was making himself man up. "I thought it was just too much trouble to you to come."

"But I didn't know you wanted me there."

"When I first bought the villa, I had visions of us sharing our time between there and the apartment."

"But then I came up pregnant and was way too nauseated to travel into the city."

"When you started to feel better physically, you never brought the possibility up."

"Neither did you."

"You'd stopped being as affectionate. I thought you were going through pregnancy stuff and I didn't want to push."

"But after I had the baby?"

"That first year, she was so fragile and tiny."

"And you didn't like to think of her in the helicopter."

"You either."

"But you used it every day to commute."

"Fear can be irrational." He sighed. "When I was with you in the helicopter, I was not afraid for your safety."

She nodded, fascinated by this insight into how her husband had thought. "Then it became habit, for us *not* to come to Athens." And that explained why when she flew into Athens with him, she was always taken back to their villa via car.

"A bad one."

"Yes, a very bad one." She had to agree. "Thank you for telling me you wanted us there. It means a lot."

"I honestly did not know it had to be said." And he was clearly uncomfortable giving voice to what he might consider needs that showed him up as weak in some way.

She wanted to reward him, so she kissed him and was totally unprepared for the tsunami of passion that would unleash.

Lying naked, sweaty and so satisfied with pleasure her body was still buzzing with it, Polly snuggled into her husband's side. "That was unexpected."

He mumbled something.

With great effort, she lifted her head and looked up at him. "What did you say?"

"You kissed me." Color burnished his taut cheekbones.

"We kiss all the time." In bed. And lately, out of it as well.

"I kiss you and you respond."

But *she* didn't kiss *him*. Emotion swamped over Polly in hot and cold waves and not all of it was good. She'd withheld her naturally affectionate nature because she had no longer been sure of him.

She'd thought he hadn't even noticed. She'd been wrong.

He'd made a lot of changes and effort in the past week; maybe it was time she did too. She could kiss him, if it meant that much to him.

Smiling she snuggled back into his side, running her hand over his chest, and reveling like she used to do in the knowledge that she was the only person with free rein to touch this incredibly powerful man like this. "I still want you to go on the walk through with me."

He made a sound that could have been arousal, or it could have been contentment, but he answered. "Surely one of your parents took responsibility for most of the house hunting."

"My parents still live in the first house they bought before I was born." She sat up, but kept her hand on him. She didn't know why, just that she needed to. "I have no idea what the process of finding a home was like for them, but my sisters and brothers tromped from house to house together."

His expression turned pained, but his hand trapped hers against his skin. "And you want to do this?"

She couldn't imagine her husband having the time for something like that. "No, as long as we go *together* to view our top three, I'll be happy."

His smile was both relieved and oh, so sexy. "That I can do."

Thinking about how much time it took to find and buy a house and how hard he had to work to make that time, she looked back on his purchase of the country villa with different eyes.

"You really were trying to do something special for me when you bought this villa."

"I was, but I see now that without your input how could this house have ever become our home?"

"That's a nice thing to say."

"I'm feeling anything but nice." He moved her hand down to the evidence of his renewed desire.

She curled her fingers around the hard flesh and gave him a heated look. "I'm not feeling so nice myself right now." She squeezed the flesh in her fingers.

He groaned. "That feels very nice to me."

And then it began again, the passion between them building to slow and easy this time as he let her touch and explore in the way that gave her the most pleasure. By the time she put her mouth on him, he was shaking and swearing though.

In Greek. He was too far gone to use another language.

She loved the earthy taste of him, the way his hardness felt in her mouth. This was her man. No one else would ever get to see him like this, much less touch him with the freedom she had to do so. Their marriage was not perfect, but this part? The passion? The desire? The way they pleasured one another?

It was as out of this world as it had been the very first time.

When she knew he was on the verge of climax, when Polly herself could take no more waiting, she climbed on top of him. "My turn."

His inarticulate sound of agreement turned her on even more.

She positioned herself over his thick erection and lowered herself, gasping as his bulbous head slipped inside her tender flesh, sensitized from their first round of lovemaking.

"That's so good," he said in a guttural tone she loved.

"Yes." She pressed down until he was fully sheathed inside her and then stilled, just savoring the amazing feeling that had not gotten old through five years of marriage and two pregnancies.

"Please, *agape mou.*"

"What? You want me to move?" Her tease would have been more effective if she wasn't so breathless and her hips weren't jerking in little tiny movements without any volition from her.

"Ne!"

Oh, yes. That was what she wanted. Polly began to move, rocking her hips, and rode him to first her completion and then only a moment later, his.

His hoarse shout was still ringing in her ears as she collapsed down onto his chest, so replete even her baby bump didn't make it awkward.

CHAPTER SEVEN

HELENA WAS ECSTATIC at her first helicopter ride. She pointed to everything out the window, jabbering away, unconcerned that her parents could not hear her well enough to answer.

But then Polly and Alexandros both smiled at their daughter and nodded at easy intervals.

Polly's eyes caught her husband's, and they shared a moment of understanding, their smiles turning intimate and warm for a moment out of time.

They landed on the helipad on top of the Kristalakis Building, Alexandros handing Helena to a bodyguard, while he personally helped Polly out and then leaned protectively over her body to shelter her from the wind generated by the slowing rotor blades.

The penthouse apartment he led them to wasn't anything like Polly had been expecting. Warm colors made the high-end rooms feel welcoming, and there was a chest filled with toys for Helena in the main living room as well as her perfect princess bedroom.

"How long has the apartment been set up for family?" Polly asked, looking around in wonder.

Helena made a beeline for the pretty white bookcase filled with her favorite stories and pulled out brand-new copies of the ones that had become dog-eared in her room in the villa. "Look, Mom! All my best stories!"

"I see that, sweetie."

Helena was in her element, but Polly was over-whelmed. There could be no question that Alexandros had gone to great lengths to make sure his daughter would be comfortable.

Polly turned and stared up at her husband. "How long?" she asked again.

He shrugged. "Pretty much since Helena's birth."

"But you never said."

"I was waiting for you to say you wanted to come."

"What? Why, for goodness' sake?" she demanded. "How was I supposed to know you wanted us here? That's not the way it seemed to me."

But the evidence of her eyes said something entirely different. It said that he *had* wanted her in Athens with him. "If you wanted us here, why did you move me out to the villa?"

"I did not realize that you would consider the move as a statement of intent."

"How was I supposed to take it?"

He grimaced, for once his ready brain stuck for an answer.

"You were waiting for me to say I wanted to come?" she asked in disbelief. "But I never wanted to move out of Athens in the first place. I would have thought that would have been a given."

Only very clearly, it had not.

"I thought you would be happy to move to the country. I thought your anger was over me choosing the house without your input. You'd made it clear you wanted to move out of the family home."

"But I said…" What had she said back then? She couldn't even remember now. She knew how she'd felt, but she'd been so angry, so resentful that by the time he bought the villa, she was halfway to closing her heart off from him already. "I really hated living with your mother and your sister."

"I am sorry I did not understand how bad it was for you."

She nodded. She believed him. She just wasn't sure if she could trust him. He was paying attention now, but he hadn't. Not then. Not later.

"I learned not to talk to you about the important stuff." She sighed and then made a conscious effort to go for the positive with a small smile. "But we're here now and it's a really nice place to be."

"I am glad you think so." He didn't look happy so much as relieved.

He wasn't used to being criticized. She'd figured that out early on. And Alexandros had been deeply offended when she reacted to his gift with anger instead of enthusiasm.

She let her smile grow. "It's a beautiful apartment."

"It makes me think of you."

That was worth a reward. She leaned up and kissed him. "I like that. Are you saying that all those nights you spent on your own up here, you were thinking about me?"

"What else would I think about?"

"Business?"

"Well, naturally without you and Helena around to keep me balanced, I tend to work very long hours." He said it like admitting a grave sin.

She just grinned and took him by the arm, leading

him into the living room, where they could sit down together. "I would expect nothing less. That's why your family is so good for you."

"You are good for me, *agape mou*. And yes, so is our daughter and this little one." He laid his hand over her belly.

The baby kicked and she grinned. "He knows his daddy's touch."

They settled onto the spice-colored sofa together, Alexandros pulling her close into his side. Neither spoke. She was basking in the present, enjoying the knowledge that she and their daughter were not only welcome here, in the bastion she had considered an adjunct to his business, but desired.

"What are you thinking?" she finally asked him after several long, peaceful minutes.

"I am enjoying your presence here in my arms and the sound of our daughter telling herself stories in her bedroom. I dreamed of just such a moment many times."

Polly didn't remind him he should have invited her if he'd wanted her there, but she did ask in a soft teasing tone, "So what have we learned about vital communication between a husband and a wife?"

"That it *is* vital." There was no humor in her husband's voice, just conviction.

"I agree. Is there anything else you've been wanting and not telling me?" she thought to ask, though with very little expectation of a positive reply.

Billionaire tycoons weren't known for not expressing their needs, or desires.

"I want to date again."

"What?" Polly pulled away so she could see her husband's face. "What do you mean? We go out together."

"To fundraisers and social functions necessary for my business."

"Well, yes, but that *is* our social life."

"I want more."

"You do?" She found that really hard to believe.

"Your sisters have date nights with their husbands. I've heard them talking about it when they come to visit."

"They do, but they don't have social calendars anything as packed as ours," Polly acknowledged ruefully. "In fact, they've all expressed envy at the galas I get to attend."

"But those galas aren't the best way to rekindle romance."

"They could be."

"What do you mean?"

"It's not about where we go, or even what we do when we are out together. It's whether we're *together* or just attending the same function."

"Of course we are together."

"Are we?" she asked, thinking how little time they actually spent in one another's company at most of the social events they attended.

He looked down at her and stopped to think, which she appreciated. He wasn't just giving her a knee-jerk reaction. "Please explain."

"On a date, your focus is on me. My focus is on you. The venue, the entertainment, the others around us, they are secondary, right?"

"Agreed."

"So, a gala could be a date, but only if our focus remained on each other."

"However, as it stands, you and I both end up talking to different people, socializing in different circles."

"Yes. You to advance your business interests."

"And you to make connections for your charity work."

"Some of the time. Others, I'm just catching up with friends," she informed him. "But regardless of our reasons, we are both in the habit of going our own way once we arrive at a function."

"That used to bother me about you," he informed her.

"What? You expected to me to stand by your side in silent companionships while you talked business and political interests related to your business?" she asked with a tinge of mockery.

But his serious nod stunned her. "Yes."

"Faithful Penelope, I am not," she informed him.

"So I learned. Not that you lack fidelity, but you do not see yourself as a satellite to my life."

"I'm not." What a strange thing for him to say.

"My mother was, to my father."

"But she has so many charity interests now. Are you saying she didn't when he was alive?"

"She did, but she still spent most of their evenings out in his near vicinity."

"I'm not sure how she managed that, but I'm not her."

"No, and I do not expect you to be."

"Are you sure?" Because that was something she'd often thought he did in fact expect and was destined to be disappointed by.

"Let me rephrase that," he said with one of his devastating smiles. "I have learned not to expect you to be. I have come to realize that if you were like my mother, I would have had no more interest in marrying you than the women she'd been throwing at my head since I became an adult."

Polly's own smile was tinged with mockery. "Sexual chemistry has a lot to answer for."

"Our relationship is not just sex." His dark gaze bored into hers.

"Of course not. We have a daughter together and a son on the way. We have a family."

"It has never been just sex." He sounded really offended.

"I didn't say it was?" she asked, rather than stated, because something she said had garnered this reaction.

"You said I married you because of sexual chemistry."

"Didn't you? I mean if we hadn't been so explosive in bed, I don't think you would have made the effort, considering our differences and your busy schedule."

He opened his mouth, like he was going to deny her assertion, but then he shut it with a snap. "That may be true, but I proposed because I was in love with you."

She'd thought so too, at the time, but Polly had long since realized what she'd thought was love was a mixture of genuine liking and sexual compatibility.

"I'm pretty sure that if you loved me, you wouldn't have been so content to be away from me so much. You wouldn't have expected me to do whatever your mother wanted, no matter how miserable it made me." She sighed and stood up, needing to put some physical distance between them. "I learned to accept that you like me. A lot. I know you're sexually attracted to me, more than you have ever been to another woman."

"I hear a but coming."

"But I think what you call love, I might call affection."

"And these emotions are not the same to you?"

"No."

"How are they different?"

"When you love someone, you consider their needs, their wants, their comfort. You want to protect them and make their life better for them."

"You do not think I feel any of these things for you, harbor any of these desires?"

"So long as you are not inconvenienced, maybe."

"But if I *am* inconvenienced, you think your needs, what you want, your very comfort becomes secondary to me?"

"Until very recently, to your mother and sister as well."

"And when I tell you I love you?"

"You haven't actually said those words very much."

"But I call you *agape mou*."

"Which means *my love*, but doesn't necessarily mean you love me. It's more like calling me *darling*."

"In some instances, yes, but not between us. Not when I say it to you."

She shrugged, not willing to argue Greek semantics. When it came down to it, it was his actions that told the real story, and until very recently the story they told hadn't been a very romantic one. She wasn't sure what they said now. Guilt? Competition with his brother? Competition with himself even? Alexandros was always top marks in whatever he did.

"But you do not believe me."

Stifling another sigh, she looked at him. "Do we really need to talk about this? Only I've really been enjoying our fresh rapport and don't want it spoiled with an argument."

"Because you know it will upset me for you to acknowledge you do not believe me when I say I love you?"

"Because you don't like being wrong. Full stop. So, if we get into this and I refuse to agree that you love me, yes, you'll become upset, but worse, you'll feel the need to convince me."

"And you don't think I can," he said in dawning understanding.

She shrugged.

"*Ohi*, say what you mean."

"Fine. No I don't. Because you think if you throw enough words at it, you'll change my point of view, only it's based on five years of your actions, and those cannot be dismissed or recategorized with mere words."

"Why not? Did we both not come to realize that you had misread my actions in not inviting you to come stay in Athens with me as I misread your actions in not coming at all?"

"If you wanted a concession in a business deal, would you expect the other party to know, or would you ask for it, demand it even?" she asked, getting irritated with him for his unwillingness to let this conversation go.

Polly had accepted her husband's lack of love and found a contentment in her marriage despite it. What right had he to stir up feelings she'd settled long ago?

"My marriage is not a business deal!" He'd raised his voice, but not to scary deep, angry levels.

Even so, Polly worried Helena was going to come searching to see what had her precious papa upset.

"No, it is not, but my point is simply that the very

fact you didn't ask for what you say you wanted would indicate that it wasn't that important to you."

"Not so important I might actually be afraid of your rejection?"

"You aren't afraid of anything."

"You are wrong about that, Polly. And you are wrong about what I feel for you." He stood up in one fluid movement and joined her, pulling her into his arms, his head coming down so his lips hovered right over hers. "If actions convinced you my feelings weren't as deep as they are, then actions are what is needed to change your mind. Not more words."

On that, at least, they agreed.

She didn't get the chance to say so because he kissed her and she fell into it like she always did. His mouth moved over hers even as he pressed his big body against her, the evidence of his arousal pressing into her stomach.

Flames of need flared through her core.

She wanted him. She always wanted him.

"Papa, you sure do kiss Mom a lot." Helena's little voice broke through the passionate haze surrounding Polly.

Polly went to jump back, but Alexandros stayed her with his hands. "Give me a moment," he practically pleaded.

She stilled and let her own breathing settle as she felt him will himself to calm down.

Polly turned her head to see Helena's sweet little face. "Are you finished reading your stories?"

Although Helena didn't actually read, she called it that when she told herself the stories from her books.

"I'm hungry."

"Then I'd say it is time to eat." Alexandros released Polly and stepped back, quickly angling himself away from their daughter. "Do you want to cook?" he asked Polly, "Or should we order takeaway?"

"If the fridge and pantry are stocked, I'd prefer to cook." Polly was warmed he'd thought to ask, because ordering delivery was what she knew his natural inclination would have been.

But Polly loved to cook. And he was respecting that reality right now.

"I left instructions for them to be."

"Good."

They spent the next forty-five minutes very pleasantly as a family while Polly prepared dinner after whipping up a quick snack so Helena would not grow fractious waiting.

In many ways, the next week was idyllic. Helena loved the penthouse apartment and because she had her people around her, didn't seem to miss the villa. A much more rested Polly got to take her daughter to the park, but didn't have to do a lot of chasing because the two nursery maids had accompanied them to Athens for the week.

While Hero had already agreed to make the permanent move to Athens, and was very excited to be able to transfer to a brick-and-mortar university, Dora was still deciding if she wanted to move out of the area where her adult children continued to live.

Polly spent part of each day on the house hunt. Some days she did actual walk throughs on promising properties and others, she watched more virtual tours, narrowing down what she really wanted in their new Athens home.

She realized on about the third day in the city that she would miss the villa. Strange and unexpected as the feelings were, Polly nevertheless acknowledged she'd made friendships in the country now too. That even the villa, for all its sterility, had been her home for more than three years and she would miss it.

She brought it up to Alexandros during dinner that evening. They were eating at a Two Michelin Star restaurant while Hero watched over Helena back in the penthouse.

It was supposed to be a date night, and Polly had taken pains with her appearance, looking forward to the evening more than she wanted to admit.

"But we discussed this. You can keep the villa. No one is saying you have to sell it." Alexandros laid his hand over hers, seemingly more interested in Polly than the gourmet food in front of him.

She'd brought up her surprising—to her—ambivalence about leaving the villa. Not because she thought they had to sell it, but because it had really surprised her that she was actually a little sad about moving to Athens. More excited than sad, but still. She hadn't expected to be sad at all, and said so.

Alexandros gave her a look that went right through to her soul. "Of course you have mixed feelings. You have strong emotions and have built bonds as you are wont to do wherever you are."

"You say that like it's a good thing." Only she could remember more than one occasion when he had derided her *deeply emotional* nature as he called it.

"I have a strong suspicion that our marriage would

not have lasted past the first six months if you did not feel emotions as deeply as you do. I have just cause to celebrate and be entirely grateful for that nature."

Out of nowhere her throat thickened and tears burned the back of her eyes. He was grateful for the soul-deep love that had prevented her from leaving him when she realized they might not be as well suited as their short, but intense, courtship had led her to believe.

She had cursed that same quirk of her nature more than once.

He reached across the table and took her hand, his eyes filled with affection. "Thank you for not giving up."

She shook her head, not wanting to cry. This was a date, darn it. Time to change the subject. "You talk like whether or not to keep the villa is all my decision." She winked at him. "It's a family decision surely."

And he'd said he'd like to keep the villa, so they could still spend time in the country as a family.

He shrugged. "It is your property."

"I was shocked when you told me that," she said with a smile.

She couldn't help wondering what might have been different for her over the past few years if she had known that from the beginning.

"So I noticed, though you must know your lack of knowledge of that fact surprised me." The waiter unobtrusively and silently refilled their wineglasses, before stepping away from the table.

Alexandros brushed his thumb back and forth across the palm of her hand, sending jolts of electric current through her. Such a tiny touch to elicit such a response in her body.

"How was I to know?" she asked, realizing how much she enjoyed having her hand in his in this public setting. It felt good. Sensual, yes, but also romantic. Though she would not make the mistake of saying so.

"But I told you when we moved in."

Confused, thinking maybe she'd missed part of the conversation while focused on the effect of his hand on hers. "Told me what?"

"That I'd bought the house for you."

She thought back to that emotionally tumultuous time and tried to remember what he'd said, certain it had not been that the house was hers lock stock and barrel.

"What do you think, yineka mou? I bought it for you."

What she'd thought had not been at all charitable, and the row that had followed had been one of their worst.

"I thought you meant you bought it for me to live in." Any other interpretation had never occurred to her.

Alexandros let out a sound of frustration. "I am beginning to see that you and I have a real problem with communication."

"You think so?" she asked teasingly.

But his expression was as serious as she'd ever seen it. "If you didn't realize the villa was yours, yes, we do."

"The prenup." To her, those two words explained her belief entirely that he would not have bought such an expensive property and put it in her name.

He gave her a pained look. "The prenuptial agreement was not my way of saying I didn't see our marriage as permanent. Nor was it intended to prevent you from enjoying the gifts I wanted to give you. It was in fact, intended to protect you as much as me, if the worst happened."

"The worst?"

"Something happened that made staying married impossible." He sighed. "It wasn't a contract intended to make you think I thought that something *would* happen."

"When I first signed it, I didn't think that," she admitted. She'd been living in a dreamworld of love at first sight, where she was his forever soul mate. "But later, after things changed between us and I realized where I fit on your list of priorities, it did seem like a pretty airtight agreement to govern the eventual and maybe even *inevitable* dissolution of our marriage."

He winced when she mentioned his list of priorities, but only said. "That is the intention of a good prenup, but I saw divorce as neither eventual or inevitable." His tone held the kind of conviction she could not simply dismiss.

His honesty deserved some of her own. "Your sister and your mom were aware of the fine details of the contract and used them to poke at me whenever the occasion arose. They wanted me to realize that you didn't see me as a permanent fixture in your life."

Rage flared in his dark gaze before it banked and only sincerity remained. "But that is a lie. I married you. I consider marriage a lifetime commitment."

Which was something they *had* discussed during their whirlwind courtship. When had she started believing other people's opinions about how her husband viewed the permanence of their marriage commitment?

Probably around the same time she realized that his mother's and sister's feelings and attitudes were more important to Alexandros than Polly's were.

He let his mother literally change her name and he'd followed suit.

"This is heavy discussion for a date night," Polly said ruefully.

"I suppose dating in marriage is a little different than out of it, but I'm still hoping to get lucky later," he teased, clearly attempting to lighten the atmosphere between them.

In the mood to let him, Polly grinned back. "I think that might be arranged...but then again, I might make you wait."

His low laughter was sexy and warm.

When they left the restaurant, Alexandros surprised Polly by taking her to a swank city hotel rather than back to the penthouse.

"What are we doing here?" she asked as he helped her out of the car.

"As much as we both love our daughter, I thought we could use a night for just us." Alexandros took Polly's arm and led her inside, bypassing the large and elegant lobby. "We have a suite on the top floor."

"Helena will be sleeping by the time we get back to the penthouse," Polly pointed out.

"Yes, but if she wakes in the night, or earlier than we do, Hero will be there for her." He smiled down at Polly with devastating charm. "While I will be there for you."

"Oh, you think I might wake in the middle of the night?"

"I plan for you to be awake, whether you will have gotten any sleep is debatable."

A frisson of anticipation zinged through Polly. "I love that tone you get."

"What tone?" he asked as he led her onto the elevator and then used his keycard to access the top floor. "The one that says I want you?"

She would have answered, but he tugged Polly into his body and covered her lips with his own, the kiss claiming and intentional and everything she loved about being the focus of this man's sexual desire.

The doors of the elevator opened a moment later, but Alexandros did not pull away. He just shifted, so she was protected in the corner as he continued to kiss her.

Polly was peripherally aware of a woman's voice and a man's low chuckle, but even knowing they shared the elevator, she could not make herself break the amazing kiss. Alexandros was not one for public displays of affection, and knowing that made the way he held her and continued to move his lips against hers, even hotter.

Alexandros moved his mouth to her ear, breathing softly in her ear and sending chills through her. "Finally. We are alone."

"We are?" she asked breathlessly.

He laughed low and husky. "Didn't you notice the other couple get off a moment ago?"

"No." She turned and nibbled that spot on his neck she knew drove her husband crazy. "Maybe I should be worried you did."

"I am always aware of our surroundings when I am with you. It's my job to make sure you are protected."

CHAPTER EIGHT

"I WISH YOU'D felt that way about your mother and sister." The words were out before she'd even thought them, old wounds too deep to ignore completely. She sighed. "I'm sorry."

He leaned back and looked down at her, his expression searching. "Why are you sorry?"

The elevator stopped and the doors opened. Polly stepped into the elegant foyer, inhaling the heady scent of jasmine as she noticed a beautiful bouquet on the marble table. "Which is our room?" she asked, indicating the four doors off the foyer.

"This way." Alexandros led her to the right and swiped his keycard to open the door.

She stepped inside, where the scent of her favorite essential oils permeating the room. Jasmine that had so delighted her when they stepped off the elevator mixed with vanilla and just the hints of orange and myrrh. It was a mix that had been prepared especially for her and that she used only in the diffuser in *her* room in the villa.

She looked around for a diffuser, but couldn't find it at first, until she realized a gorgeous clay pot glazed in deep blues and browns had mist coming from the stylized top. "Where did you get my aromatherapy mix?" she asked, a little awed.

Yes, he was a billionaire. Yes, her husband was scarily efficient, but to have gotten her scent he had to have noticed it that *one* time he'd been in *her* room.

It was the kind of attention to the tiny details in relation to her that he had shown when they first got together, but much less frequently since marriage and her move to Greece.

"I asked the housekeeper at the villa why your room smelled so perfectly like you."

Polly smiled, flattered he considered the delicious blend of scents as much *her* as she did. "That diffuser is a work of art."

"Literally. I contacted an artist you like and asked if she had anything that could be made into a diffuser."

"When did you do that?"

"Last week."

"She worked fast."

"She had the art piece. It was just a matter of installing the water chamber, etc."

"For a date night?" she asked, just a little stunned.

"For a gift. I thought using it tonight would make the gift more special."

Polly couldn't help herself, didn't even want to. She reached up and hugged him exuberantly and kissed him the same way before leaning back. "Thank you. It's lovely."

"I am glad you like it. Now, why were you sorry in the elevator?"

Polly sighed and then grimaced. "We're having such a nice date. I don't want to ruin it."

"That is the second time you have said that. Believe

me when I tell you that the only thing that would ruin this date is if you were to leave."

"I'm pretty sure you wouldn't be thrilled if we didn't make love." She would not be keen on such an outcome either.

"I love your body, my dear wife, but even if you were not to share it with me tonight, I would still count myself a very lucky man to be here with you."

"You used to say stuff like that all the time." She'd noticed when he stopped.

"And you used to kiss and hug me several times a day." He had noticed when she'd stopped too.

Was it possible he'd felt something of the insecurity that had plagued her when their relationship changed?

"Hugging and kissing you isn't a hardship," she offered before doing both again.

He kept her close and deepened the kiss when she would have pulled away. Somehow she found herself sitting on a cream sofa in front of the fireplace in the sitting area, making out with her husband. He did something with one of his hands and then the fire flared to life and Polly couldn't help smiling.

"You know how much I love a fire in the evening." Not that fires were necessary but a few nights a year in the Mediterranean climate.

"I'm in all-out seduction mode, if you hadn't noticed." He said it lightly, like he was teasing, but something in his gorgeous espresso gaze said he was entirely serious.

"Let me let you in on a secret, Alexandros. When it comes to you, I'm a sure a thing."

"That is good to hear, *agape mou*, but I have learned

not to take anything about my very precious wife for granted."

"You're turning into quite the romantic." And she really didn't care if that was prompted by his need to prove he was as good a, or better, husband than his brother.

His smile flashed, his entire face covered in happiness.

But before she could ask him why he seemed so happy, he kissed her again. This time, hands came into play. Dragging an inciting hand up her leg and her inner thigh, and cupping her breast with his other hand, his thumb playing over her already stiff nipple, Alexandros seemed intent on driving her insane with need before they even got their clothes off.

He teased reactions from her body like a man who had spent years studying it, like she was the specially crafted instrument and he the prodigy who would spend the rest of his life playing it.

Not a passive lover by nature, Polly gave as good as she got, touching her husband as only she was allowed to do. That truth had never gotten old. She was way more possessive than she ever thought she would be, but in his way, Alexandros was too.

One thing she never worried about was that he would have a roving eye. Because, like hers, his possessive streak was accompanied by a bedrock of loyalty that would not be shaken.

Needing more intimacy than they could achieve with their clothes on, Polly sat up and shook her head. "Stop for a minute, Andros."

Her husband went so still, she wasn't even sure he was breathing.

"I didn't meant freeze." She laughed. "Just get your clothes off."

"The love, it is still inside you. Perhaps buried very deeply, but still there."

She wasn't having some heavy conversation in the middle of sex. Not today. "Get naked." When he still didn't move, she said, "Please."

"Say it again and I will do whatever you wish."

"Say what again?" she demanded, ready to recite the alphabet in both English and Greek if it meant getting his suit off.

"Call me Andros."

Nonplussed, she stared at him. He was serious. She wasn't sure why it was so important to him that she call him by the nickname she'd once used exclusively, but she wasn't about to say no. Not if it meant getting what she wanted.

"*Andros*, take off your clothes."

He shuddered, like she'd touched him in the very way she was longing to do. "*Ne. Ne.* Anything you want, *yineka mou.*"

He stood up and stripped out of his suit before she even got the zip undone on her dress. Lately she wasn't keen on zippers, but when she knew her evening would end with her husband, that was something different.

He loved unzipping her, and she loved how he kissed her nape and between her shoulder blades when he did.

So why was she even trying to undo the zip herself?

Because she wanted naked. Now. Only... Maybe she still wanted that little bit of pampering too.

"Could you?" She meant to turn and offer him her back but the view of his body arrested all movement on her end.

She loved the olive-toned skin that rippled over muscles honed by a strict workout regime some athletes would find it difficult to maintain. But Polly's husband never did anything by halves. He had to be the best at whatever he did.

Which meant he'd worked out his training schedule with a trainer who also served top echelon athletes.

The results were fantastic as far as Polly was concerned, both because she loved looking at her husband's amazing body but also because she knew he was taking care of his health.

Ensuring he would be with her and their children for a very long time to come.

But that amazing body that turned her on so much?

Also served as a reminder of how important it was to Alexandros to be the best. Not second, and definitely not a poor shower, especially, she thought, when compared to his brother.

"Stop," he instructed.

"Stop what?" she asked.

"Whatever you are thinking. Just stop thinking it."

A small laugh huffed out of her. He was so arrogant, thinking he could dictate even her thoughts, but in this instance? He had a point.

"I want you." She would always want him.

"I am so hungry for you I'm not going to get your dress off if we don't get that zip down now," he told her, his voice a near growl.

Shivers of desire and atavistic need skated along her every nerve ending.

Polly shifted so he could reach the zipper. Finally.

If she didn't know better, she'd think his hand trembled against her as he tugged the zip down, but there was no mistaking the sucking in of air as he exposed her back. "I would love to take time to appreciate the beauty of this sexy bit of lace holding your gorgeous breasts in, but it will have to be another time."

He undid the clasp and pulled the fabric aside before placing a kiss on her spine. But it was the kiss on her nape, the one she'd been waiting for that made her shudder with need.

"You are so perfect for me. So responsive."

"Yes." The one thing they'd always gotten right was their perfect physical response to one another.

He brushed her dress down her body, letting it pool at her hips as he slid his hands back up her torso to cup her breasts. Polly was so sensitive that she moaned at the contact. Alexandros brushed his thumbs over her turgid nipples and the sound that came out of her was far more animalistic.

"Yes, play with them, Andros!" she demanded.

"Like this?" he asked, pinching her nipples with just the right amount of pressure.

Each press of thumb to forefinger matched a pulse of pleasure in her most intimate place.

"So good!" She loved touching him, but sometimes she enjoyed him playing her body like the sexual virtuoso he was to her.

Alexandros began tugging her nipples and rolling them in between the simple moments of pressure, and pleasure built in Polly as if he was caressing her clitoris. "I'm going to come like this," she warned him, unable to believe she was so on edge.

Polly pressed her thighs together, sending sparks of ecstasy through her core, but it wasn't enough.

"Andros, please!" She wanted. She needed. She was in an agony of pleasure not quite fulfilled.

"Then, come for me, *yineka mou*. Show me what my touch to your body does," he coaxed against her ear, hot air sending more chills of pleasure along her body.

"I…" She moaned. Words were too hard.

He pinched just a little harder on her nipples, his hard sex pressing against her back, his need clear, but he made no move to stop doing what he was doing.

"Inside!" She shifted her pelvis, seeking more touch between them. "I want you inside."

"I thought you wanted it like this," he said gutturally.

"Inside!" she demanded again.

He didn't make her beg, but lifted her so her dress could fall to the floor. Her and Alexandros's fingers tangled in the attempt to get rid of her panties, but neither laughed.

He grunted, she mewled with need and the lingerie was on the floor with her dress.

Then he lifted her, and she spread her legs, knowing what he wanted. Alexandros lowered her until his leaking sex kissed her tender flesh. She pushed down so his head pressed inside.

He let her take him at her own pace, though his body was rigid with the effort.

Finally he was in, filling her intimately as no other man ever would do, as no other woman would ever feel him. They rocked together, chasing pleasure, seeking that ultimate moment of completion.

Usually in this position, he reached around to touch that special bundle of nerves, but he continued his ministrations to her breasts and nipples. And that was all she needed.

Overwhelming pleasure spiraled inside her, built even more quickly by how his hardness caressed her G-spot.

"That's right, *agape mou*. Move on me like I am all that you need."

"You are," she gasped out, her breath coming in harsh pants.

"And *you* are all that *I* need."

The words sent her careening into the ultimate pleasure, her body convulsing around his, a shout of intimate joy coming out of her. He pressed his mouth into her neck, his movements growing jerky, and then he let out a guttural groan against her neck, his own climax making that big body under hers go rigid.

Afterward he carried her into the shower, a decadent tile enclosure easily big enough for the two of them. They washed each other, their knowledge of the other's body not making the exercise any less special or enticing.

When he lifted her and carried her dripping wet to the bed to make love again, she could only ask him to hurry.

This time, he took his time, building the pleasure between them until they were both sweaty and shaking with need. When they finally went over, she thought she'd sleep on the damp sheets and not care, she was so wrung out from pleasure.

But Alexandros ran her a bath and then joined her after calling housekeeping to come change the sheets while they were in the bath.

"Nice to be a billionaire," she slurred sleepily, lying against him in the softly scented water.

"Even nicer to be your husband." His tone was intense, like he wasn't joking.

She was too tired to figure out whatever message he was trying to give. "I'm not changing the sheets." She yawned. "Be lucky if I make it back to the bed."

"Do not worry, *yineka mou*, I will take care of you."

She patted his chest. "Nice husband."

Dozy, she didn't catch what he said.

They soaked for a while before he lifted her lax body from the water. Alexandros helped her dry before drying himself and then carrying her to the freshly made bed.

The following days were idyllic. Like she'd always dreamed her marriage would be.

Alexandros was back in the penthouse every evening by six. They ate dinner early together as a family before he helped her put Helena to bed. He usually spent an hour or so on the computer in the evenings, but Polly understood his multibillion-dollar company demanded more than a nine-to-five effort from its head. They didn't watch movies on the sofa together, but Polly usually ended up sitting, leaning against him as she read or worked on recipe ideas in her notebook.

Alexandros had joined Polly and Helena for lunch twice, which she'd loved and so had their daughter. Polly and Alexandros had curtailed their social obligations in ways she'd never believed he would be open to.

They had only attended three high society functions, and Polly was thriving under the less demanding schedule.

She felt better than she had since getting pregnant. No longer exhausted, she reveled in the time she had to spend with her daughter, exploring the child-friendly parks and attractions of the ancient city.

Polly loved it all, but there was a little place in her heart that didn't trust this new lifestyle to last.

That same place made her put off any concrete actions looking for a house in Athens. She kept looking at videos the estate agent sent her and passing on likely candidates to Alexandros, but Polly avoided in-depth discussions about the potential properties, and while she'd gone to visit a couple, she had not asked Alexandros to join her.

She could not help wondering if they lived somewhere not quite as convenient for her husband as an elevator ride away, would she and their daughter see him nearly as much?

They had been in Athens two weeks when Alexandros brought the house hunt up as they relaxed together in the living room after putting Helena to bed together. He was on his computer, and she was continuing to catch up on her reading list, their silence companionable.

So she was startled when he asked, "Are you really finding it that difficult to find a house that will meet our needs here in Athens?"

She laid her books aside and stared at him, trying to assemble her thoughts without sounding like the untrusting wife she was. "Um, no, of course not."

"I thought you'd love that house in Palaio Psychico." He mentioned one of the properties she'd gone to view in person.

A gorgeous, newly built house with a pool that was half indoor and half outdoor, a play area already prepared for children with a climbing structure with slides and swing. The architect had designed rooms and a layout that felt comfortable. It was the best candidate so far for something Polly would consider a family home, not just a showplace.

"Your sister would have kittens if you bought me a house in the most exclusive neighborhood of Athens." Which was not an answer.

His expression said he recognized her misdirection for what it was. "Since when do you care what my sister thinks?"

"You don't like upsetting her. Or your mother," she reminded him, in case he'd forgotten.

Life had gotten very strange in past weeks.

"In case you have not noticed, I have learned my lesson in that regard."

"I, yes, I'm sure. Lesson? Why are we talking about your family?" Only she knew why. She'd brought them up.

Would Polly *ever* learn *her* lesson in this regard?

Alexandros set his computer aside and shifted Polly from her comfy spot beside him to his lap. Feelings that had nothing to do with house hunting sparked through her.

"You are babbling, *yineka mou*. Why is that, I wonder?"

She shrugged, much more interested in the feel of his hard thighs under her bottom than their current discussion.

He laughed. "Hold that thought and answer my question."

"What question?" she asked, her thought train derailing on a tide of lust.

He cursed. "You are too delectable, but we are not ignoring our relationship for sex this time."

"Isn't sex part of our relationship?" she asked as she shifted and sighed with the decadent pleasure of his nearness.

He kissed her like he couldn't help himself, the passion between them building fast. She was working on the buttons of his shirt, wanting skin, when his hand stilled hers.

"Stop," he ordered gutturally. "I mean it, Polly."

She smiled at his use of her name and not the despised Anna. "I don't want to stop."

"We'll make love."

"Of course we will." It was the one part of their marriage they got right.

She didn't realize she'd said those words aloud until he lifted her from his lap and placed her back on the sofa. "And maybe that is part of the problem, *agape mou*."

She frowned, still not always comfortable with his use of that particular endearment and more than a little unhappy about the physical distance between them he had created. She would feel rejected, but the bulge in his slacks proved he was as turned on as she was.

Only he wanted to talk.

And Polly? Really didn't. Talking wasn't all it was cracked up to be.

But the stubborn expression on his face said Alexandros wasn't letting this go.

Feeling vulnerable in a way she hadn't in a very long time with him, Polly crossed her arms over her chest and settled back against the sofa, doing her very best to give the impression of a woman who could take or leave lovemaking. "I would say it's a very good thing."

After all, if they weren't so good at the intimacy part of their marriage, she wasn't entirely sure their marriage would have survived the first year. That didn't make her feel proud, but it was a truth she could not ignore.

"It is a wonderful thing," he assured her.

"And yet you are over there." She indicated the other end of the sofa with a wave of her hand. "And I am here."

"Do not pout. This is important, I think."

"I am not pouting." Maybe.

His smile was indulgent, but the expression in his espresso gaze was serious. "Our marriage has been broken for a very long time, and I did not realize it because I am blessed with a wife who is generous and beautifully passionate in bed."

"What are you saying?"

"Why haven't you asked me to look at any of the house options here in Athens?" he asked, showing he had that trick down too.

She shrugged. "Are we in a rush to find a house?"

"You are less than three months away from giving birth. I would say so, yes."

"But we don't have to move before the baby is born."

"Why wouldn't we?"

"Maybe I like living here in the penthouse. Helena is happy here."

"She would be just as happy in a house with a garden to play in."

"We have the roof garden." It had a pool as well, and she and Helena got their daily dose of swimming just as they had at the villa. There was room for a play structure up there, but she didn't know how Alexandros would feel about changing the look from elegant showpiece to family friendly.

"You want to stay here?" he asked, surprise lacing his tone. "We could turn the guest room into a nursery, I suppose." He frowned as if in thought. "I imagined you'd prefer to have more room."

She laughed, the sound harsher than she would have expected. "Helena and I used maybe four rooms in the villa when you weren't there."

He grimaced, acknowledging a truth he'd been ignorant of until very recently. "Because it felt too much like a hotel to you."

"Yes." She sighed, deciding to be honest, even though she wasn't sure about revealing her thoughts and fears to the man she had learned not to trust, but had never stopped loving.

Whoever said there could be no love without trust didn't understand the nature of consuming love.

Of course, she'd prefer to trust her husband with her heart, but she wasn't going to stop loving him just because she couldn't.

She took a deep breath and let it out slowly. "Cards on the table?"

"That is one of those American idioms you are so fond of, isn't it?"

She rolled her eyes. And he accused her of going off on tangents. "Yes, it means—"

"That you will show me your thoughts you've been hiding. Yes I know."

"I'm not hiding anything." She sighed. "Not on purpose."

"What have you been hiding *not on purpose*?" he asked.

"Okay. First of all, you realize that this penthouse has more square footage than the house I grew up in?"

He inclined his head, waiting, she was sure for her to get to the point.

"My parents raised four children in that house."

"So, you want a smaller house?" he asked, sounding like he was trying to figure out what she was saying.

"Not per se, but this penthouse has four bedrooms. Yes, one is set up as an office that we can both use, so that's nice."

"You are rambling again."

"I'm not. I'm explaining."

"I apologize. I am listening." He made the gesture she'd taught Helena to indicate turning her listening ears on.

Polly smiled. "Good. We don't need a guest room. We can put my family up in either the corporate apartments, when they come to visit, or a hotel if you have business associates using the apartments on the next level down."

"Business associates or out-of-town employees can use a hotel in that case. Family always comes first," Alexandros declared.

"That's great. I'd rather have Mom and Dad closer when they come to stay especially."

"But you do not want a house that could accommodate this?" he asked.

"I like the penthouse. I like especially that it's so easy for you to come home to."

Understanding flared in his gorgeous gaze. "You

think if we buy a house that will require any sort of commute that I will not come home as often?"

"Yes. Even Palaio Psychico would require a fifteen-minute drive in good traffic." If they moved there, her super busy tycoon husband would have no hope of popping in for lunch when his schedule had an extra hour in it.

"And that is thirty minutes more than you want to spend away from me each day?" he asked, sounding pleased rather than like he thought she was needy and demanding.

Which gave her the courage for honesty. "Closer to an hour with you coming home in congested traffic, but yes."

"And perhaps you are worried that if I have to work late into the evening, I will be tempted to stay here rather than drive to our home?" he guessed.

She shrugged. They both knew that was more probability than possibility.

"I assure you that it would never happen."

That was nice of him to say, but she had her doubts.

They must have shown on her face because he frowned. "In essence, you do not want to pick out your dream home here in Athens because you do not trust me to place a priority to spend time there with you and our children?"

He wasn't sounding so pleased now.

"You're a workaholic, Alexandros. Pretending otherwise won't change the truth."

"I explained that."

"You explained not being around for my first pregnancy. And I understand it now, even if I wish you'd been forthcoming at the time. But Alexandros, you have *always* worked long hours. Since our move to the villa, you spent at least one night *every* week here in the penthouse. Sometimes multiple nights."

"That cannot be true." Now he was giving her the look, the one that said she was too demanding and needy.

Polly pulled her defenses around her, reminding herself this was why she could no longer trust him with her love. "If you don't believe me, look at your pilot's log. It will show you the truth."

He grabbed his phone, she was sure, doing exactly that. He no doubt thought he would prove her wrong, but his expression changed to one of chagrin as he read the pilot's log.

She waited in silence for him to acknowledge the truth.

He put the phone down, his expression easily read. Her super smart, super competitive husband did not like being wrong.

"Well," she prompted.

"Not every week." He sighed. "But as good as. And I now realize I spent multiple nights here in the penthouse far more often than I should have."

She said nothing. She'd known that. She hadn't needed to read the pilot's log. Why? Because she had missed Alexandros when he was gone. Obviously, he had not been as afflicted, not even realizing how much time he spent away from her and Helena.

"Nevertheless, a fifty-minute helicopter ride is not the same as a fifteen-minute drive," he claimed in the growing silence between them.

"But an unnecessary commute, in any case."

"We cannot do the type of entertaining expected of a man of my stature in the penthouse."

"We still have the villa. We can continue to entertain there when necessary and host the local events at the same facilities we've used in the past."

"But that was when our home was in the country. We are talking about my family living full-time in Athens."

"So, buying a house here in Athens is about your consequence?" she asked quietly, not surprised, but a little disappointed by that fact.

He stared at her. "That is not what I said."

"Isn't it?"

"Are you picking a fight?"

"Disagreeing with you is not me picking a fight, Alexandros. Neither is me asking you a legitimate question."

He surged up from the couch, anger making the lines of his gorgeous face harsh. "So once again I am the big bad billionaire?"

CHAPTER NINE

Inappropriately, Polly wanted to laugh.

But he had the look of a sulky boy, and she just knew he wouldn't appreciate her saying so.

"You may be big," she teased, indicating a certain part of his anatomy with a significant look. "And there is no question you are a billionaire, but I never said you were bad."

"You did. You said I am a bad husband."

She opened her mouth to deny, but realized she *had* said that, or as good as. "You've improved loads," she offered.

"And let us not forget I perform well in the bedroom," he said angrily.

She blinked at him, not sure what to say. Alexandros was happy to go head-to-head with power players, but he'd never liked arguing with her. If she gave him an out, he always took it.

Always.

For some reason, this time, he was forcing the issue, refusing to brush uncomfortable feelings back under the carpet.

"Please remember that I want to live here so your children and I can have more time with you. This is not me saying you are a bad husband." That was absolute truth. "It is me saying I want our marriage to work. If you're serious about fixing the brokenness, then so am I."

The anger drained away, but the expression it left behind was more sad than relieved. "I must cling to that truth, I suppose."

She put her hand out, asking silently for help standing. Not that she couldn't get up on her own, but it was harder now and she wanted the physical connection.

He immediately took her hand and leaned forward to slide a hand around her waist before smoothly pulling her to her feet.

"Thank you." She made no move to put distance between them. "Is it really so important for you to have a showcase here in Athens?"

He leaned his forehead against hers, not speaking for several seconds.

She didn't push.

"No. It is not, but the idea that you don't trust me to change...that hurts."

"I am sorry," she whispered, unable to deny the lack of trust.

"Me too."

She didn't ask what he was sorry for. Was he sorry she didn't trust him? Was he sorry he had destroyed that trust? Did it matter?

They made love that night with a tender desperation, both needing the connection of their bodies to affirm their merged lives.

The next day Polly chatted with Corrina about her desire to continue living in the penthouse apartment.

"You and Petros seem more than happy living here," she pointed out.

"And I wouldn't mind staying indefinitely." Corrina paused and then shrugged. "If some changes were made to make this area more family friendly."

Polly looked around the perfectly manicured container garden on the roof, the furniture that was designed to impress business associates and even the pool that didn't have a rail on the stairs going into the shallow end for children to hold on to.

"You know your husband actually owns the Kristalakis Building, not the corporation? I asked and Petros told me." Corrina smiled at Helena's antics in the pool. "Your daughter is so sweet."

Polly smiled. "I like to think so."

Their younger nursemaid, Hero, was swimming with the three-year-old, looking like she was having as much fun in the water as the toddler.

"Anyway, the company could easily buy condos or use hotels for corporate guests, and the family could reclaim the floor below our places," Corrina suggested. "The apartments could be remodeled to accommodate the security team as well as a playroom for the children and suites for family guests."

Polly frowned at the work that would take, but was unable to dismiss the idea entirely. "That would be a pretty big undertaking."

Corrina shrugged with the insouciance of someone born to wealth. "It's not as if you'd have to put up with the mess. They wouldn't be touching our apartments. You know?"

"But..."

"And we could wait to do the remodel until after

your family visits for the baby. Until then, the security team and family can use the apartments as they are."

"I like the idea of indoor play area for the children."

"The roof garden isn't exactly practical on the hottest days of summer for anything other than swimming, but we're going to have to install some shading up here. I've wanted some for a while. And that area over there would be a great spot for a play structure." Corrina indicated the center of the roof. "We don't need to get rid of the helicopter pad, just shift to the spot they land and put up a wall with a locking gate for safety's sake."

It would be the safest and easiest to oversee spot, but it would definitely change the roof to family focused rather than business impressive.

"You've been thinking about this."

"I want children someday and I don't want to move into the family house, Polly."

"But Petros would buy you your own home."

Corrina didn't look too sure about that. "Maybe. Maybe not. He's really struggling with the family schism that's happening right now."

"Is he?" Polly felt badly, knowing that schism was between *her* and her mother- and sister-in-law.

"Yes." Corrina reached out and patted Polly's arm. "Don't get that look. I mean it. This is not your fault. It is Athena's and Stacia's fault. They're both way too used to getting their way with Alexandros and Petros. Trust me, I wasn't putting up with Athena manipulating my marriage, much less that little madame, Stacia."

Not like they'd manipulated Polly's. Polly got that. Still. "You're everything Athena wanted in a daughter-in-law."

"Don't you believe it. Women like that are never

happy with their daughters-in-law. They want to be the center of their sons' lives."

"No, I'm sure Athena wants both her sons to be happy. She just doesn't believe Alexandros can be happy with me." As hurtful as her mother-in-law's behavior had been for Polly, she had never felt the other woman was purely selfish.

Not like Stacia.

"More the fool her. No one else could have given Alexandros what he needed in a wife. Only a blind person would think differently."

Uncomfortable with that declaration, Polly fell back on humor. "We're very compatible in bed." She waggled her brows suggestively and both women cracked up.

"What is so funny?" Petros asked, sliding onto the seat beside his wife.

"Papa! Uncle Petros! Look how fast I swim!" Helena demanded from the pool.

"Is something wrong?" Polly asked Alexandros as he settled into a matching chair kitty-corner to Polly's.

It was midmorning, nowhere near lunchtime.

"No. Why should there be?" Alexandros's expression chided her.

Because it was work hours and he was there, with them, not in his office doing stuff to take over the business world? She didn't say that, realizing from his expectant and not altogether pleasant expression, he was just waiting for her to say something of the sort.

Not sure why he was suddenly spoiling for an argument, Polly just gave him a sugar-sweet smile. "No reason."

Her husband's dark gaze narrowed. "A meeting got

canceled and I decided to spend my suddenly free hour with my family."

"Well, I'm glad you did," she said sincerely.

And that was one more reason staying here in the penthouse was a good idea. Apparently if they were close at hand, Alexandros would opt to give his family these unexpected moments rather than work.

Even if that only happened occasionally, it was worth it.

Alexandros clapped along with his brother in appreciation of Helena's swimming efforts.

"Well done, poppet," Polly said to her daughter with a big smile.

"Now that smile is genuine. What do I have to do, I wonder, to earn that kind of warm approval?" Alexandros said, his voice low and sensual. "Or do I already know?"

Polly looked over at him, realizing what he was implying at the same time as she caught that even if his brother had not heard what she'd said to cause her and Corrina's laughter, her husband had.

And while his tease had been all sexual innuendo, there had been an angry edge to it Polly did not understand.

But she got it later when they were readying for bed, and it appalled her. "You want to do what?" she demanded, making no effort to modulate her tone to something resembling calm.

"You are convinced the only place I value you is in the bedroom. I think we should take a break from sex while we work on other aspects of our marriage."

"Whose idea was this? Have you been talking to your mother?" she demanded.

"I have in fact, but it wasn't her idea."

"I bet. She convinced you it was your idea, didn't she?" Athena had tried suggesting the no-sex thing once already, ostensibly for the sake of Polly's health during her pregnancy.

"My mother feels badly for all she has done to undermine our marriage and the ways she hurt you, even when it was entirely unintentional."

Unintentional? "Did you just imply your mother did not mean to undermine our marriage? That there was something accidental about her assurances that our marriage was a temporary aberration in your life and the prenuptial agreement was proof?" she asked in a dangerously controlled voice.

Alexandros didn't appear worried. "She misunderstood the prenuptial agreement as much as you did."

"Oh, did she? And why is that?"

He tugged at the collar on the shirt he had yet to remove in preparation for his shower before bed. "The agreement my father had her sign was materially different."

"It was?" Polly asked in a flat tone, never having considered that possibility.

"It was a different time."

"Was it?" Or had his father simply trusted his wife more than Alexandros had trusted Polly?

Another possibility sent a hollow feeling through Polly. Maybe subconsciously, Alexandros *had* considered their marriage temporary. But then Polly had gotten pregnant and their marriage became a permanent fixture in his life, one he could never admit to himself, much less anyone else that he had ever seen in a different light.

"You know, Alexandros, I'm done fighting your mother's machinations. You want to sleep separately while we *work on* our marriage? Be my guest." She pointed to the closed door, her message clear.

"I did not say we should sleep separately."

"You said we shouldn't have sex." And if he thought that was possible while sharing a bed, he'd lost his mind.

"Well, yes." Though he wasn't sounding so confident about that little detail.

Right at that moment, Polly did not care.

She went into the closet and came out with a suit, shirt and tie for him to wear the next day. "Take these to the guest room. I'll get your underthings and you can grab your stuff from the bathroom."

"What? I'm not moving out of our bedroom."

"Yes. Yes, you are."

He took the clothes from her but shook his head. "No, that is not what I meant."

"Neither of us can sleep in the same bed without touching each other. I choose not to be teased by what I cannot have. Ergo you will be sleeping in the guest room."

"But that is not what I want."

"Tough."

He stared at her like she was the unreasonable one. She didn't care. She was just done.

"Get out, Alexandros. I need my rest." She placed her hand protectively over her stomach, not even a little ashamed to pull the pregnancy card.

She'd had two difficult pregnancies and very little in the way of accommodation for them.

She'd spent so long not giving in to her own limitations for his sake and the sake of peace between them, but she was done with that too.

For once, Polly was going to insist on what she wanted, what would be easiest for her.

His male pride and ego could go hang.

He'd promised her he wouldn't let his mother, or sister, come between them, but here he was doing just that. All the anger that Polly had tamped down for five years of marriage was sizzling through her bloodstream like lava, the volcano of her fury so close to eruption, it was all she could do not to scream.

"You said we get along in bed," he said, like that should explain everything.

"And you said you want to give that up to focus on other areas of our marriage. I guess we'll see just how good you are at doing that, won't we?" she asked with a snide tone she wasn't proud of, but neither was she shouting at him.

So, there was that.

He drew himself up like her words had firmed his resolve. "Yes, we will."

"Well, then…" She indicated the door with her hand.

He frowned. "We can still share a bed."

"No, we cannot. You want no sex. I want to sleep alone. Deal with it."

"Polly you should not take this as a rejection."

"Don't worry, that's not how I see it."

"I want to say that's good, but your tone implies it's not."

"Alexandros, I'm done talking. Please leave."

He opened his mouth but then shut it as if her words

had finally registered and he had decided to respect her desires.

With a final look at her that she could not read and didn't really care to, Alexandros turned and left. He was back moments later to retrieve the pile of remaining things he'd need for the morning that she'd gathered.

She waited until he was finished in the bathroom before going inside to take her evening shower, ignoring his quiet *good-night* as he left the room.

If a few angry and pain-filled tears mixed with the water, there was no one else there to see.

Alexandros flopped to his side, missing his wife's form in the bed next to him more than he would have expected, even though this sleeping arrangement was not what he'd been angling for. After all, sleeping on his own in the penthouse wasn't something new for him. But he could not get comfortable.

He wasn't so stupid he even tried to tell himself it was the bed. He missed Polly and couldn't help feeling he might have made a huge tactical error.

The conviction that Polly believed the only thing they had between them was sex had grown day by day. She'd said it more than once.

Bed was the one place in their marriage that they got it right.

He was too much of an overachiever to accept that kind of limitation. He wanted her to trust him. To believe he loved her.

He didn't want her to think his words of love were just a mix of affection and lust like she'd said they were.

He loved her madly, deeply and forever.

No way could he accept that view.

And he was at a loss as to why she could not see the truth.

Yes, he'd made some mistakes. Loads of them if he were honest, but he'd shown her his love too. Okay, yes, they struggled with communication. Yes, she'd misunderstood some things, but enough to believe he didn't know what he meant when he told her he loved her?

It made no sense.

Alexandros had given more to Polly than he had to any woman that had come before her.

He had made her his wife. He had changed things in his life to make her happy.

Only somehow, he had failed.

And failure did not sit well with him.

He *would* prove to his wife that he loved her and didn't just lust after her. Though that emotion was strong enough.

He hadn't argued with his banishment to the guest room for two reasons.

One, his wife was angry with him, but it was the look of wounded vulnerability he could not argue with.

And two, she had been right. If he slept with her in his arms, he would have touched her. And if he touched her, his good intentions would not have stood against his physical need for her.

Maybe he needed to prove to both of them that lust was not the basis of their marriage.

He knew she thought his mother had instigated this, but Polly was wrong on that count. Every time his wife had implied their compatibility in the bedroom was their saving grace, he'd grown more and more bothered.

And determined to prove her wrong.

His mother had told him that if he wanted to fix

what he had broken, he would have to sacrifice his own wants and desires.

He could not think of a bigger sacrifice than to give up sex with his wife while he proved himself to her.

But lying there in the dark, craving her touch, just wanting to hear her breathing beside him, he had to question his own wisdom.

Perhaps he could prove his love without giving up the one thing they got right.

Maybe he'd been a world-class idiot giving that one thing up when there was a very real possibility it was the *only* thing that had kept his marriage together at times.

The thought chilled him and made it no easier to sleep.

Alexandros heard his wife moving around as soon as she got up.

Though she was quiet, no doubt not wanting to wake their energetic daughter, he was aware of every rustle that indicated Pollyanna was no longer sleeping peacefully in their bed. If she had slept peacefully at all. He certainly had not.

The prospect that his request the night before had given his wife as poor a night's rest as he'd had did not sit well with him.

Skipping his usual workout, Alexandros was even more efficient than normal with his morning ablutions, finishing his shower quickly and dressing without fuss. Alexandros left his suit jacket off until after breakfast as was his usual habit and went in search of Pollyanna.

She wasn't in their room or the kitchen as he'd expected her to be. She baked when stressed and he'd half expected to walk into controlled chaos, but the kitchen was pristine. A quick search of the apartment and their personal terrace only revealed his still-sleeping daughter in her room.

He opened the door to the foyer. No Polly.

But their security guard was in his usual place.

"My wife?" Alexandros inquired.

The guard nodded toward the ceiling. "Up on the rooftop."

"Alone?" Alexandros barked.

He tried to let Polly have as much normalcy to her life as possible, but she was the wife of a billionaire. Alone was not a word she got to indulge in.

"No, *kyrios*. Sanders is up there watching her from a distance."

Trying to give his wife the illusion of privacy. Alexandros approved.

Alexandros nodded his acknowledgment before knocking on the door of his brother's apartment. Petros was dressed to work out, as Alexandros had expected he would be. They both started their days early.

"I need you to keep an ear out for Helena while I talk to Pollyanna."

His brother didn't ask why, or suggest they talk later, just nodded his head and made his way into the other penthouse apartment. Knowing his daughter was in good hands, Alexandros headed up to the roof.

Sanders stood unobtrusively in the shadows, and Alexandros dismissed him with a quick hand gesture.

Pollyanna didn't seem to be aware of Alexandros's presence, her focus on the budding sunrise. Ensconced on the designer outdoor sectional the decorator had assured him was perfect for the space, her feet tucked under her, she held a steaming mug.

His wife had not dressed, but merely pulled a wrap on over her pajamas. It was a homey look that she made altogether too enticing.

"*Kalimera*, Pollyanna."

She looked up, no surprise evident in the smooth movement, her expression serious but lacking the suppressed fury that had been there the night before.

In that moment, he did not know if that was a good or bad thing.

"Good morning, Alexandros. I see you are ready to face your day."

He shrugged. It would never occur to him to come out onto the rooftop garden half-dressed, much less in his sleep shorts and T-shirt.

It was one of the ways they were very different. He did not have the luxury of presenting any appearance but absolute control.

He settled on the sectional as well, rather than taking one of the armchairs. "How did you sleep?"

She gave an almost smile. "You know? Surprisingly well. I was so angry you were listening to your mother about our marriage again, but suddenly I was just tired. And I slept."

He winced. That didn't sound as promising as it should have. Tired of him? Tired of trying? Tired of what?

"My mother told me that if I wanted to fix what *I* had broken, I had to be prepared to sacrifice my own wants and desires. I could imagine no greater sacrifice than to give up the physical expression of the passion between us, though I honestly believe she had no idea

I was thinking about how sex seemed to paper over cracks I hadn't even known were there."

Pollyanna studied him, like she was trying to read his mind. Maybe she was. "Really? At the villa, you know what she said."

"I do, but it is very possible a woman of my mother's generation actually believes that forgoing intercourse during pregnancy is what is best." That she felt the need to offer that advice was something he still found difficult to fathom.

But then Pollyanna had not been looking in the best of health the last time she saw his mother and sister before the visit to Villa Liakada.

His wife inclined her head. Not an agreement, but not a dismissal either.

Her ability to be fair, even in the face of great provocation was something he should *never* have dismissed when she asked for his support against his mother and sister.

Alexandros had been unable to get past the *against* concept, never taking the next step to realizing how very necessary presenting a unified front had been and how very much his wife had deserved his support. Full stop.

"I told her that if I lost you because of her and Stacia, I would cut them both from my life permanently." It was very little in the way of reparation for past mistakes, but he offered it with absolute sincerity.

Surprise flared in Polly's beautiful blue eyes. "Did you mean it?"

"I did." That she even felt the need to ask increased his anger with himself.

He should never have made her doubt her importance to him or where his ultimate loyalty lay.

"I appreciate that you feel so strongly, you would say something like that, but let's not pretend. No matter what their machinations, if you lose me Alexandros, it won't be *their* fault."

Tension thrummed through Alexandros, his jaw tightening so it was hard to speak, but he managed it. "I know."

"You're the one who broke promises to me, who told me he loved me and then treated me like I didn't matter too many times to discount." She'd said things like this, back when they were first married. She'd said them with tears and she'd screamed them.

And he had not listened.

He was listening now, though his wife's voice was void of emotion.

Alexandros gritted his teeth against a sound that wanted to come out of his own aching throat, the back of his eyes burning with impossible moisture. "I am sorry."

"I wonder. Are you sorry? Do you believe you were genuinely in the wrong, or are you simply trying to prove that your brother is not a better husband than you?"

"Is that what you think this is about?" Alexandros asked, unexpected pain ripping through him.

Alexandros was not an emotional guy. He couldn't afford to be.

"Yes." That was all.

Just one word given in a flat tone from his overly emotional, voluble wife.

No overexplaining. No tears. No glaring.

He did not like this lack of emotion in her. One way

she'd always been his complement was that Pollyanna could give voice to feelings he could not even admit having to himself.

"It is true. I do not like thinking you see my brother as a better husband to his wife than I am to you. I am a competitive man," he admitted, wondering for the first time in his life if perhaps that trait was not always a good thing.

Her lips twisted. "I know."

Of course she did. Pollyanna knew him well, whereas he had lost sight of who she was and needed to learn her heart all over again. "I find it far more disturbing that you would consider me a poor husband at all, if you want the truth. I'm sure you think that's very conceited of me, but you are the best wife I could ever imagine having." He still marveled at the miracle that had them meeting. "That I would not be the same for you is not something I can accept."

"That may change."

He knew she wasn't talking about him becoming her ideal of a husband. She didn't believe he wanted that role badly enough to change. She was talking about her being his perfect mate. "I assure you, it will not."

"I'm done making all the compromises," she said in a tone that warned him more was coming. "For the next little while, I think I may be done compromising at all."

"Tell me what you want, and I will see you get it." It was another promise, but she would learn this one wasn't empty.

"Even if it means I want six months to build our relationship without your mother's or sister's influence?" she asked, her voice laced with doubt in his sincerity.

CHAPTER TEN

ALEXANDROS'S KNEE-JERK REACTION was to deny such a thing. What would his father have said?

However, he'd just promised he would give his wife what she needed so they could work on their marriage.

He could make the same choices he always had in the past and expect Polly to go along with his family's norms, or he could do something different. Something that proved she mattered more than anything or anyone to him.

"You do not want to see my mother at all, even at our son's birth?" he asked, rather than reacting with his first instincts. His mother would be devastated. "What about her seeing Helena?"

"I will not allow our daughter to be hurt," Pollyanna said, as if that should be obvious.

"Then what?"

"I trust Corrina to supervise visits with your mother."

"And the birth of our son?" It was only ten weeks away, give or take.

"I don't want your mother or your sister anywhere around me during that time." The implacability in Pollyanna's manner could not be ignored. She wasn't going to move on this matter. "I don't want them visiting me, or our baby in the hospital."

"My mother will be very hurt." He wasn't going to argue with his wife, but he needed to point out the consequences of such a course of actions.

Pollyanna's wry gaze said she was fully aware. "Tell me something, Alexandros. If a company that relied on your goodwill did everything it could to undermine you in the market and talk Kristalakis Inc. down, what would you do?"

"Destroy it." He sighed, fully aware of how quickly and unhesitatingly he had answered. "But this is family, Pollyanna, not a business rival."

"I didn't say a rival. I said a company that should be your ally, but for reasons of their own decided not to be."

He nodded, acknowledging the point.

"And I don't want to *destroy* your mother, but I do want her to stop and think about the cost of her behavior. If I had left you as she wanted, I would have raised Helena in America and this baby would never have come to be. Athena would rarely have seen her granddaughter and she never would have gotten the chance to know her grandson."

All the air whooshed out of Alexandros's body. "You are not leaving me." He swallowed back the tightness in his throat. "*Please*, do not leave me."

"I have no plans to do so, but if your mother had gotten her way, I already would have."

"She didn't believe you were the right woman for me." Alexandros had no choice but to acknowledge that.

His mother had baldly admitted as much to him when she'd come to his office to apologize.

"That implies she's had a change of heart."

"She has."

"I hope that's true, but my six-month moratorium stays. And I don't want you seeing her either."

"What? You do not mean that."

"I do."

"But Polly, my father is gone. It is my duty to look after my mother." He could not abandon the older woman entirely, no matter how angry she made him.

Which said what about the threat he'd been so sure he meant about cutting her out of his life if he lost his wife?

"Your brother can do the looking after for a while. I don't want to wonder if your actions are driven by your own feelings or hers. I want a chance to get to know each other again without poisonous whispers making things that should be beautiful ugly."

Pollyanna leaned toward him earnestly. "I believe if we are both willing to work at it, if we truly do focus on our marriage for the next six months, then maybe you'll be in a place where you won't put her feelings above mine and maybe I'll be in a place to trust you not to."

There was that word, *trust*. The one thing besides her love that Alexandros most wanted from the beautiful, vibrant woman he had married.

"Petros was very smart to move into the penthouse after marriage, wasn't he?" Alexandros asked ruefully.

He'd thought his brother had been wrong to refuse to postpone his own wedding on their mother's whim; now Alexandros realized just how wrong he'd been about so many things.

Pollyanna relaxed back against the sofa, taking a sip of her tea. "I think he learned from our mistakes."

"You mean *my* mistakes."

"No. I didn't argue moving in with your family and

then it took me a while to realize your mother's and sister's behavior was intentional."

"Because you could not imagine my mother and sister trying to break us up. Your family would never do something like that." And she hadn't argued moving in because her tender heart had been moved by the losses his family had suffered and his mother's plea they all continue to live together at the villa as a family.

As generations of the Kristalakis family had done.

"No, they wouldn't. My mother? She despised my oldest sister's husband when they first married, but she never said a word against him."

"How did you know she despised him?"

"I didn't like him either, and I went to my mom for advice. She told me it didn't matter if we liked him, my sister loved him."

"But you like him now."

"I do. So does Mom."

"What changed?"

"The easy answer? He did. We did. The hard one? My sister got ovarian cancer. It's a terrifying disease that kills more women than survive it. My sister survived and a lot of that is down to how well he took care of her. He found an experimental treatment program in Canada, and even though they told him there was no room for my sister, he wouldn't take no for an answer. He got her in. That pushy certainty he was always right saved my sister's life, and I learned that he loved her as much as she loved him. Just because he wasn't touchy-feely and had a sometimes acerbic sense of humor didn't mean his emotions weren't just as engaged. Mom and I love him now."

"My mother thinks you are a saint." His mother had

spent their time apart as a family doing some soul-searching of her own, and she had admitted to Alexandros she hadn't liked what she'd found.

"In six months, she can tell me that herself if she really thinks it." Again, there was no give in Pollyanna on this.

"I wouldn't lie to you."

"On purpose, no, I don't think you would."

"But unwittingly, you think I would."

"Something like that."

"What else?" he asked, more than a little worried what other "un-compromises" his wife wanted.

"I want to stay in the penthouse."

That, at least, was easy. "Done."

"Corrina thinks we can convert the corporate apartments into more usable space for visiting family, our security team and some kind of indoor playroom-slash-gym for the children."

"Whatever you want."

"I want this space to be family friendly." She indicated the rooftop garden with an all-encompassing wave.

"What does that mean?"

Pollyanna listed some things she and Corrina had brainstormed the day before.

"I will find a nearby building to move the helipad to. I would prefer a more parklike setting for our children." Which would require the entire space of the rooftop.

If they were going to live in a penthouse, his family was going to have the best that lifestyle had to offer.

"Are you sure?" Pollyanna asked, as if she really thought he'd balk at something so simple.

"You could have asked me for any of this anytime

in the past five years, and I would have done it," he assured her.

"Maybe you actually believe that, but I know it's not true."

"I can prove nothing about my intentions in the past, only the present. Know those intentions are for your contentment."

"Not happiness?"

"No one person can assure another's happiness."

"I agree."

"You chose to be happy while living under the strain of a life not anything like what you'd wanted or imagined you would have with me." He understood that now. "I believe you will find it much easier to make that choice if you are genuinely content with your lot."

She took another sip of her no longer steaming tea, the scent of chamomile wafting to him. "You're probably right."

"I like to be right."

"I know." A worried expression flitted over her lovely features, but then it was gone. "I'm not going back to full-time corporate prop after the baby is born. I want time with my children."

"You seem much more relaxed with the current schedule." And it bothered him more than she would ever understand now that he understood how much she had not enjoyed her previous one. How exhausting she had found it and how she had tried so hard to be the attentive parent she wanted to be and still not let *him* down.

"I am."

"Then we will keep it."

She stilled, like she was waiting for him to take the words back. Of course, he did not.

Finally, she nodded. "I would like that."

"Corrina and Petros can do some of the socializing for the company's sake we have been doing these past five years."

"So, you won't just start going to these things without me?"

"Ohi." No, he would not. Absolutely. Did she not realize he would miss her? But he did not say so, only offered what he knew she would believe. "I too want to see my children grow."

"I'm glad." Pollyanna untucked her feet, no doubt preparing to stand. "Well, that's a good place to start, don't you think?"

"I do." He reached for her tea and took a sip, grimacing at the taste.

She smiled. "Not your favorite."

"No, but you like it."

"I do."

"And that is all that matters." He hoped she understood that he was talking about more than tea here.

"Is there anything you want to see happen?"

That she would even ask proved to him once again how committed to making their marriage work his incredible wife really was. "Your generosity of spirit humbles me. Since you are asking, date nights. I want them once a week, whether we've been to a business-related social function, or not."

"I'd like that, Alexandros." She stood, clearly assuming he was done.

But he wasn't. "I want to call you *agape mou* without you flinching, frowning, or turning your face away."

"I…" She let her voice trail off and showed she understood how important this was by really thinking about her answer. "I'll try."

He nodded. "About last night—"

"As angry as you made me, I think it's a good idea," she slotted in before he could tell her he'd been stupid to suggest such a thing.

"You do?"

She nodded.

"For six months?" If his voice rose on the word *months*, he could be forgiven.

"No. The six months is about your mother and sister only. I'm due in ten weeks and then six after that while I heal."

"That's still four months," he practically shouted.

She startled, like his raised voice had surprised her. "It was your idea."

"And it was stupid."

"No. You were right. We both used sex to paper over the cracks. I don't want those cracks becoming chasms."

He wanted to argue, but Alexandros found he could not. He had let his wife down in a very real way. If this was his penance, then he would pay it.

"You want to go shopping? With me?" Polly wasn't sure she'd heard her husband correctly.

It was just not *him*. The Alexandros Kristalakises of the world did not trail along with their wives to the shops.

His smile was all warm engaging charm. "You may have not noticed, but you are expecting our son in just over two months."

"Hard to miss." Harder to miss was that it was midmorning and her business tycoon husband was in their penthouse, not his office.

Again.

"We have no nursery for him."

They did have a nursery. At Villa Liakada. "We have everything at the villa." She should have had the nursery furniture, the bassinet at the very least, brought to Athens.

Polly wasn't sure why she hadn't already taken care of it. The entire layette she'd put together for her son's arrival was still in there as well.

"Which we will need when we are staying there on weekends."

"Papa!" Helena came careening into the living room, Hero close in her wake. "Are you going to go swimming with us?"

"Not today, *louloudi mou*. I am taking Mama shopping."

His *little flower* made a face. Helena definitely took after her father in her lack of interest in that pastime. "Do I have to go?" the three-year-old asked suspiciously.

"*Ohi*. You will go swimming with Hero, have a lovely lunch with Aunt Corrina and then take your nap, *ne*?" They were going to have to hire a second nursemaid to replace Dora in Athens.

The older woman would keep her position on a part-time basis for when they visited the villa, but she hadn't wanted to make the move to Athens.

"I get to visit Aunt Corrina?" Helena asked excitedly.

"Most assuredly, but only if you promise to nap nicely for Hero afterward. She has schoolwork she has to do."

Polly smiled her approval at her husband remembering what to him was probably trivial, but was very important for Hero. "You're a very nice man for a billionaire business shark."

"I am glad you think so." His smile had a spark of something that sent need sparking through Polly even as their daughter promised most sincerely to take her nap nicely.

Hero and Helena, accompanied by two of the security team, left for the pool a moment later, and Polly was left alone with her confusing husband.

"You want to furnish a nursery? But you're sleeping in it." Had he forgotten that salient fact?

"I live in hope my wife will invite me back into our bed, sex or no sex," he said, his voice low and seductive, his body somehow closer than he had been only a second ago. "Until then, we can have a daybed installed in the office."

There was certainly room for one. One thing about the penthouse was that the rooms were all oversize. There was enough square footage for six bedrooms easily, but the architect had designed the apartment on a grand scale, every room oversize with lots of built-in storage.

Her husband had been overstating the case when he said they didn't have the facilities to entertain. Parties of fifty or more? Would be crowded. But their dining table could be extended to accommodate seating for ten.

When it was kept in its current formation for six, there was more than adequate space for hosting a cocktail party comfortably, even if they didn't have a banquet-size room like they did at Villa Liakada. And while it was nowhere near the size of the rooftop garden, their personal terrace was quite large and well situated to increase their entertainment space.

"I did not kick you out of our bed. It was a mutual decision, based on your suggestion, I might add." She missed him in their bed.

Of course she did, but not having sex to fall back on as a distraction tactic was forcing them both to be more forthcoming and maybe even more aware of the other's needs outside of the bedroom. She'd realized how much he enjoyed her company when it didn't lead to sex, how important it was to him to spend time together, regardless.

She liked knowing that, but also acknowledged that there had been many times in the past she had unknowingly disregarded his need for her companionship, thinking it was all about the sex.

"One I regretted almost immediately, but even so, I think it has been illuminating in a good way for both of us."

His words so closely resembled her own thoughts, Polly smiled. "I think so too."

"That does not mean I want this moratorium to last indefinitely." He said it like she might actually be thinking along those lines.

"Neither do I," Polly assured him.

"Good." He leaned down and kissed her.

Polly responded, letting her body relax into his.

Alexandros took her weight, sliding his arm around her expanded waist. When he pulled his mouth from hers, they were both breathing heavily, but there was no urgency to take things further. It felt too good just to be held, to be needed for more than her body.

That thought hit her hard. Did she think of herself

that way? Had he been right that Polly had stopped believing in the romance of their relationship? That he
cared for her as more than a convenient, if very compatible, bed partner?

"So, you want to go shopping?"

"I've cleared my schedule for the rest of the day."

Wow. She shifted so she could meet his eyes. "The
whole day?"

"We don't have to shop the whole time," he said,
sounding just the tiniest bit panicked.

Polly laughed. "We don't have to shop at all. We can
order everything online."

"You don't like ordering personal things online, unless you have no choice," he said, showing a perception she would not have expected, but more than that,
a consideration for her feelings that she'd learned not
to expect either.

The fact her newly perceptive husband realized just
how personal the nursery was to her touched Polly
deeply.

"He's going to sleep in our room in the bassinet for
the first few weeks," she reminded Alexandros.

"I remember Helena. I thought your mother and mine
were going to come to blows over your refusal to put
our newborn in the nursery at night."

"Just because she doesn't choose to voice her opinion
over all her adult children's decisions, doesn't mean she
can't hold her own when she needs to." It had helped that
in that case, Alexandros had not sided with his mother.

Polly had told him flat out that he could move out of
their bedroom if he didn't like the baby's bassinet being
in there. But he'd told her he had no problem with it.

He had adored their daughter from before her birth.

"Not that she liked her bassinet at first," Polly remembered fondly. "She only slept well when you held her on your chest." The nights he'd spent in Athens away from them those first two weeks had been rough.

Helena had eventually settled into her bassinet and not needed her daddy's heartbeat in her ear to sleep.

"I remember. It was a special time."

Love for this man poured through Polly, and she smiled at him. "Yes, it was."

They shopped high-end boutiques for nursery items and additions to the baby's layette, but then Alexandros instructed their driver to take them to a store on the outskirts of Athens.

They hadn't found a crib and changing table yet, though Polly had seen a couple that would work. Just nothing that she'd fallen in love with. "Where are we going?"

"You'll see."

"I don't like surprises."

"That is not true."

She laughed. "No, it's not, but I still want to know."

"Are you hungry? Would you like lunch first?"

Her tummy rumbled, answering his question.

His laughter was rich and warm, and she couldn't help what she did next any more than she could have stopped taking her next breath.

Polly leaned over and kissed him, not rushing it. Letting her lips move against his, loving how he returned the caress instantly but made no move to take it deeper.

Finally, she pulled back only far enough to look into his eyes. "Thank you."

"You are welcome, but why are you thanking me?"

"For taking this time, for doing it with a smile and that super sexy laugh that makes me all warm inside."

"I'm very glad to know my laughter affects you that way."

"It's more than that, it's knowing you're happy to be here."

"I am."

She didn't remind him there had been a time when he wouldn't have been. They were going forward, not staying mired in the past. "So am I."

They ate lunch on the patio of a café that served traditional Greek fare. Polly enjoyed her spanakopita very much, but kept snacking on the pistachios on the crudités plate.

She ate the last one and frowned.

"Would you like me to get you more?" Was that laughter in his voice.

Polly blushed. "I don't know why, but I've just been craving pistachios this pregnancy."

"No doubt your body needs the nutrients found in them."

"Or I just love their salty goodness."

"Or that." He laughed, but waved a waiter over and requested more for their table.

"I'm going to turn green if I keep eating these," she joked.

"Even green, I will still love you."

Polly went still, his words doing things to her heart and emotions, not all of them good, but mostly good.

"You've never been a guy who says that a lot." And she'd finally decided it meant he didn't feel the emotion like she did.

It hadn't been like that in the beginning of their relationship. She hadn't needed the words as a frequent affirmation. But that was before they meshed lives that she now realized had probably never been meant to go together.

He acknowledged her words with an indecipherable look. "I have come to see that not saying the words may have convinced you they were no longer true."

If they ever had been. "If it had just been a matter of saying it, or not saying it, I don't think I would have drawn that conclusion." Her dad adored his wife and children. However, he had never been a man to make a lot of verbal declarations. "But it isn't, is it?"

"What do you mean?" His gorgeous face revealed a confusion that might have annoyed her weeks before.

She'd thought he should *know*, but now she saw it as more endearing. He was trying.

"If you had shown me that you loved me, if I had been a priority in your life," she explained, "I don't think the lack of words would have bothered me. It might other women, I don't know. I only know myself."

"And you needed actions I did not give, so the lack of words cemented a belief inside you that I do not love you."

"Yes." It was a level of honesty they did not usually engage in.

But there was no moving forward as they'd both said they wanted to do without putting truth out there to be dealt with.

He nodded. "It is my intention to both say the words and to show you that I feel them."

She wanted that, more than was safe for her heart.

"This *reconstruct our marriage* plan is a risky one, you understand that, don't you?"

"I would have said not to do it was riskier."

"But I'd settled into our marriage, found my peace with the limitations of our life. You're doing your best to convince me that we can have something different, something better. If I believe you and you let me down, I don't know if I have what it takes to find that peace again." Simply admitting that was scary for her, because it meant her future might take a turn she did not want, had never wanted, but might not be able to avoid.

"Is that why you are fighting this so hard?" he asked, as if he was finally understanding something that had bothered him.

But she didn't understand his question. "How am I fighting it?" She'd agreed to try, hadn't she? Agreed to work toward an emotional intimacy she'd blocked herself off from since before the birth of their daughter.

"You do not trust me to change."

"Well, no." But that wasn't fighting against him trying to, was it?

He winced, like he'd really hoped for a different answer. "Because you fear that if you trust me and I let you down again, it will be the end."

She laid her hands over her stomach, letting the life there give her a measure of peace. "Yes."

"And you do not want that?"

She shook her head. "We have two children together." She didn't want to bring their son into a broken home.

Alexandros nodded. "Both our daughter and our unborn son deserve the strongest family we can give them."

"And in your mind, that means having a strong marriage?" She'd thought he believed that, when they'd first dated and gotten married.

Then she'd come to believe Alexandros had very different priorities than building a strong marriage with her.

"Ne." He infused that one word of affirmation with a deep sense of feeling and commitment.

And she liked hearing it. A lot. This bid of his to save their marriage wasn't only about his need to prove he was as good a husband as his brother.

"You know, our marriage wasn't rocky." Not until he'd started pressing her for things she no longer felt able to give. Like her trust.

"How stable could it be if you were not as happy in it as I was?"

"From my perspective, it was very stable."

"Only because you never considered the possibility that if you no longer loved your husband, you could fall in love with someone else." He said the words like even voicing the thought pained him, but it was a real worry for him.

She would never have expected him to entertain such a thought. "I would not allow a relationship to develop to the point that might happen." And she'd never fallen out of love with *him*, so it was a moot point anyway.

She was terminally afflicted.

"I believe you would not knowingly do so."

"But you think it *could* happen?" she asked, still surprised he harbored such a worry.

"I think I will never take that risk."

"Staying married is really important to you." Had it always been? Polly didn't know.

Wasn't sure it mattered. It was true now and that was what was important.

Pain flared in his espresso gaze. "It is, and I am sorry you came to believe otherwise."

"I'm not sure how much I *believed* and how much I *feared*. And once I got pregnant, well, I never even considered you'd end things between us."

"That is something at least."

"Family is important to both of us."

"Yes, but perhaps I put too much emphasis on my family of birth and not enough on the one I was making with you." It was a huge admission for a loyal Greek son and brother to make.

"If you want to visit your mom, you can. I should never have made that a condition of—" Polly paused, trying to think how to put it "—whatever this is between us."

"You are very tenderhearted."

"I just know how much it would hurt me not to talk to my mom or siblings for the next few months. And you have always adored your family. It isn't fair of me to make you choose between me and them." Even temporarily.

"Like they tried so very hard to do?"

He was admitting it? "I thought you'd convinced yourself your mom's machinations were unintentional?"

"I realize now my mother was utterly convinced our marriage could not work and that ultimately I would not be happy in it, but I do believe some of the hurt she dealt you was not on purpose. Only the result of her natural arrogance."

"Like mother like son," Polly teased.

"No doubt. You should have met my father, but I

think if he had lived you would have had a very different welcome from my family."

"You think he would have liked me?" Petros liked her. He always had. Maybe their father would have too.

"He would have loved you and the way I became a better person with you in my life."

"What an incredible thing to say. You believe that?"

"I know it," Alexandros said with full sincerity. "Thousands of employees have kept their jobs over the years of our marriage because when I took over their companies, *you* were my conscience."

"Really?" He thought about her at work? That in itself was a revelation.

"Absolutely. Ask Petros if you do not believe me. My policy for dealing with mergers and takeovers took a sharp turn after our marriage."

"Why?"

"You don't remember your lectures on the importance of the individual?"

How could she forget? She'd found his willingness to listen to her take on philosophy and human interaction as heady as their sexual combustibility. "I thought you were indulging me. I didn't think you were *listening*!"

"Didn't you?"

"Maybe at first," she admitted. And she'd liked it, the possibility that she could influence someone so powerful because of his affection for her.

"I did listen and I did change." He looked at her like he wanted her to hear the unspoken message behind those words.

He was listening to her now, and he was trying to change.

Polly didn't stifle her urge to touch him as she might

have done recently, but reached across the table and brushed her fingers over the back of his hand. "Noted."

Alexandros's smile was brilliant. "Good."

"I should have realized you were building walls around your heart." The lines of his face moved into a serious cast. "At first, though, I was just relieved you had stopped arguing about every little thing."

He sounded ashamed of that fact.

"You don't like being in conflict with me." Recent willingness to the contrary.

He grimaced, looking a little ashamed. "It makes me feel powerless."

How could this man ever feel powerless? "I would have said that you had all the power to bring peace between us."

"Not when I was just waiting for you to settle into our life." His wry expression acknowledged that might have been a shortsighted attitude.

But suddenly she wasn't feeling as much bonhomie as before. "You thought I'd get used to being dictated to by your mother and mocked by your sister?"

He grimaced, his shrug almost self-effacing. "That was not quite how I saw it, but yes."

"In a way, you were right. I did make my peace with our marriage," she acknowledged.

"By relegating me to a place outside your heart, I would have said even outside your intimate circle, but—"

"There was still the sex." And that sex had made him think things were fine and allowed her to pretend they were too.

He winked, a bit of his usual arrogance flashing. "Very good sex."

"Terrific sex," she teased back and then sighed as the brief flash of humor faded. It was time for more honesty. "Emotionally, you *were* outside that intimate circle."

He nodded. "You stopped trusting me with anything but your body."

Polly had no reply. They both knew it was true, but hearing the words hurt.

Both of them, if his expression was anything to go by.

"I'm not going to see my mother, or my sister, until you are ready to see them too," he announced, like he was making a major concession.

Anger gripped her and she gasped. "That's not fair."

"How?" he asked, looking genuinely confused.

Could he be that dense?

"Because I'll feel pressured to see them, so you don't suffer the loss of them in your life."

"I do not want you feeling pressured, but surely you realize my family has to mend bridges with you as well." He sounded so rational, so pragmatic.

But he was once again ignoring every need Polly expressed and putting the needs of his family ahead of her. Or at least, that's what it felt like.

Filled with unexpected fury, Polly surged to her feet and tossed her napkin on the table. "How about we see if we can even mend the broken bits between *us* before you start pressuring me into making happy families with the Kristalakis Harpies?"

Instead of being offended, or even miffed at the unflattering distinction, Alexandros threw his head back and laughed. "Harpies they might be, but they are still your family, *yineka mou.*"

But Polly wasn't feeling the humor and shook her

head firmly, her frown severe. "Oh, no, they are not. I married you, not your family and if I *never* want to see either your mother or your sister again, then that is my prerogative. And I'd believe you were really changing in your attitude toward me if you had come to that conclusion on your own."

She turned and headed toward the street, knowing the car would be called, if not by her husband then by security. No one wanted her wandering off.

That had been drilled into her from the beginning. And maybe just this minute she was acknowledging a certain level of resentment because of it.

When she'd first come to realize just how much her life and personal freedom had changed, Polly had told herself she had to just deal with it. She had fallen in love with a billionaire and married him. Her choice. So, she had to accept the good with the bad.

And if there seemed to be more bad than good, well, it had still been her choice.

Only it hadn't been an informed one.

How could it be? Polly had never had any experience with the kind of life the truly wealthy lived.

And Alexandros had made no effort to warn her in advance. Not of any of it. He'd expected his mother and sister to help Polly navigate her new life, but they resented the heck out of his new bride and just wanted her gone.

Polly had been so focused on him and what Alexandros made her feel, she'd never considered how much her life was going to change. That she would never again be able to wander the streets of a downtown, or go to a mall alone to shop, walk and think.

Never be able to take her children for a walk in the

park without security, would have to look for hidden motives in overtures of friendship.

Wouldn't even be able to cook in her own kitchen anytime she wanted.

Once her children were old enough, they still wouldn't be able to stay with her parents for a week in the summer. Polly's mom and dad's humble home didn't have the security measures to keep her children safe.

Who was Alexandros to tell her that, on top of everything else she'd had to give up in her life as his wife, she had to claim his mean-spirited and manipulative sister and mother as *her* family?

Not in this lifetime.

Suddenly he was there, right beside her, his arm offered. "Come, let us finish our shopping."

She jerked a nod but made no move to take his arm.

The silence that reigned in the car was not the companionable silence they'd shared so often the past week. Tension thrummed between them. Polly had no desire to dispel it and ignored any efforts her husband made to do so.

CHAPTER ELEVEN

ALEXANDROS'S SURPRISE FOR Polly turned out to be a shop for a master carpenter who specialized in baby furniture.

Pushing away negative thoughts and feelings, as she'd learned to do, Polly ignored the presence of her husband and allowed herself to enjoy the beautiful handmade pieces.

She found a crib in dark wood and matching dresser with a changing mat on top. The old-world style charmed her, and she started asking the sales associate about the construction and adherence to safety guidelines.

"All my furniture meets the strictest safety guidelines because I ship internationally." The deep, pleasant masculine voice had Polly turning.

"You made all this?" she asked, with a little awe, indicating all the beautiful pieces in the showroom.

His smile was warm, and understandably proud. "I did."

"How? I mean…"

"My grandfather was a master carpenter. He had me in his shop when I was a small boy, learning to sand and oil wood."

"And you followed in his footsteps?"

The man nodded.

"That's so neat. I started baking with my grandmother and became a pastry chef."

"I am sure your grandmother was very happy to see her skills living on in you."

"As your grandfather must be."

The man's smile slipped a little. "We lost him in my teens but when I am in my shop, making furniture for the next generation, I feel his presence and know he lives through my memories."

Polly blinked back tears. "That is beautiful." She wiped at her eyes. "Sorry, I'm that typically emotional pregnant woman."

"I think perhaps you are a sensitive soul, pregnant, or not." He went to offer her a handkerchief from his pocket.

But her husband's hand was there first, his crisp cotton square shaken out for her.

She grabbed it and dabbed at the moisture. "Thank you, Alexandros."

"*You* are Kyria Kristalakis?"

"Yes, she is my wife." Alexandros inserted himself between them, forcing the carpenter to take a step back.

Looking far from intimidated, the man winked at Polly. "Your husband is feeling protective."

Polly looked up at Alexandros, not really understanding where all this testosterone posturing was coming from. "I guess." She shrugged and looked back at the carpenter. "I would really like this nursery suite. Is it available?"

"For you, I will have it delivered this week."

Alexandros growled, the sound primal. "We can find our furniture elsewhere."

"No, we cannot," Polly informed him, enunciating each word so there could be no misunderstanding. Then she smiled at the master carpenter. "I would love if you could have it delivered this week. We're getting a little close for comfort."

"And you did not even want to go shopping today." Alexandros sounded almost petulant.

But billionaire tycoons didn't get petulant, did they?

She rolled her eyes at him. "I never said I didn't want to go shopping, I said I was surprised you did."

The shop owner laughed and, showing he had some self-preservation, asked Alexandros for the details for delivery. But then he smiled at Polly. "Do you have a bassinet?"

They'd bought one earlier that morning and she said so.

He shrugged. "Okay."

"But you have one you think my wife would like?" Alexandros asked, as if the words were being pulled from him.

"It is in the same style as the crib and dresser changing table."

"Oh…" Polly wanted to see it. She really did, but she'd already gotten one, and that would be silly. Wouldn't it?

"Show it to us," Alexandros instructed.

"Please," Polly prompted his good manners.

Her husband frowned down at her, but said it.

"She has you wrapped around her finger, doesn't she?" the master carpenter asked Alexandros as he led them across the shop and into the back room.

"She doesn't think so."

"Is she blind?"

"Sometimes."

Polly ignored them both for the gorgeous bassinet in the center of the room. "Oh, it's stunning." It had wheels, so she could move it around the penthouse as needed.

In the same old-world design as the other pieces they were buying, the beautifully stained dark wood gleamed with the love and care that had gone into making it.

"Have it delivered along with the other pieces." Alexandros took her arm to lead Polly away.

She balked at moving. "But we already have a bassinet."

"I will have it returned."

"But…"

"You want this one and I want you happy."

"It's just a bassinet."

But it wasn't. It was Alexandros telling her she didn't have to settle. Not now. Not ever?

Or was she reading too much into a simple furniture purchase?

They were back in the car, moving slowly through the packed Athens traffic when Alexandros reached out to take Polly's hand.

He squeezed it and then brought her hand to his lap, absently brushing his fingers over hers. "I am sorry, *agape mou.*"

His use of the endearment sounded very intentional.

Polly turned so she could see his expression. "Why sorry?"

He was looking at their hands together, like the sight held the answers of the universe.

"I was Cro-Magnon man in there. Isn't that what you call me?"

"On occasion."

"I don't like other men flirting with you."

"I never noticed that before." It was an inevitable reality at so many of the functions they attended together. Polly had never been particularly comfortable with the social flirting but had noticed early on that it was common.

Thank goodness her husband had never indulged. She never would have been sanguine about it.

And Polly never flirted back, but she had always been cordial.

"I never doubted before." It sounded like a hard-fought admission.

One she would not ignore. "What are you doubting now?"

"Your love. My right to it. Whether you will stay with me." His shrug was more bleak than negligent.

"Have I ever once threatened to leave?"

"No, but you said earlier that what we are doing right now, all this honesty, it is risky."

She nodded. "Okay, so that made you feel insecure?"

Polly expected him to deny it. He was too arrogant to feel insecure.

But Alexandros nodded. "*Ne.* Though, if I'm honest I haven't been feeling all that secure with you since that dinner with my family."

"The one where you decided I thought your brother was a better husband than you."

"The one where you said as much."

She was going to argue, but he'd taken her words to mean that so there was no point belaboring what she'd actually said.

"I would have thought that the knowledge I'd stayed with you despite it all would have given you more confidence. Not less."

"What man wants to believe his wife stayed with him for the sake of their child? Not this man." He spoke the last with a lot more force than she'd been expecting from his subdued demeanor.

"I didn't just stay with you because of Helena." Yes, Polly's first pregnancy had played a pivotal role in her decision to accept her life and stop beating against the walls of his indifference to her needs. But... "I loved you when I married you. I loved you when I got pregnant with Helena." She took a deep breath and went for full disclosure. "I love you now."

"Perhaps you do, but you are no longer in love with me. The stars..." He stopped, swallowed, then continued. "They are gone."

His voice came out thick with emotion.

He'd said something like that before, but he was wrong. "Alexandros, when we are at Villa Liakada there are so many stars in the sky, it is like a blanket of twinkling lights." She scooted as close as she could get to him with her seat belt. "Here in Athens, the stars are still beautiful, but there are a lot less of them."

Polly brushed her hand over her husband's bowed head. "Or are there?"

He stilled, but didn't answer.

"Just because we can't see them for the light pollution, doesn't mean they aren't there, Alexandros. Every star we can see in the country is still in the sky in the city."

"What are you trying to say to me?" he asked in a thick voice.

"Alexandros, the stars are still there."

Hot moisture splashed on the back of her hand.

Shock rendered her mute for several seconds but then another drop of moisture landed on her hand.

"Alexandros?"

"How can the stars be there?" his words came out choppy, tinged with emotion she had never heard from him before.

Even the day he'd proposed.

He'd been all arrogant certainty she'd say yes that day. And she had.

But right now? He was hurting. Hurting like she had never thought he could hurt because of her.

Polly said the only truth that mattered right then. "I love you, Andros."

A sob snaked out of her powerful husband, then he was clinging to her while his loss of composure sparked her own. They held each other, a watershed of emotion pouring over them both.

"I love you, Polly, *agape mou*. You have to believe that. I need you to believe that."

She didn't answer. She couldn't. She believed he loved her. She couldn't not, but what did that mean?

For him? For her?

Because if he'd always loved her, then what did that say about how easily he dismissed her feelings before?

"We need…" He paused like the words were too hard to find.

"What?" she prompted. "What do we need?"

"A place to talk where we will not be interrupted and where I can hold you properly."

"Another hotel suite?" she said, teasingly, trying to lighten the mood a little.

He shook his head, his demeanor entirely grave. "This discussion is too personal for any place but our home."

"Okay."

He nodded. "Okay."

He released her with one arm, but kept the other around her while he grabbed his phone and texted someone. A few minutes and several texts later, he said, "Done."

"What?"

"Petros and Corrina will keep Helena tonight."

"That's kind of them."

"Petros has an interest in us working through our problems."

"He does?" Well of course he did. Petros loved his brother and he loved Polly like a sister now too.

"Yes," Alexandros said grimly.

"Okay, well, it's still nice of them."

"It is, yes," he admitted grudgingly. "Another instance where my brother is showing his *considerate* nature."

"You can be really caring and considerate too, Andros."

"Do you think so?" He didn't sound like he believed she thought anything of the sort.

"It may have taken you five years to get there, but once you realized what your mom and sister were like with me, you put a stop to it. Once you realized I wanted to see more of you, you took steps to make that happen."

"That doesn't make me considerate. That makes me a desperate man who does not want to lose his wife."

"But you *can* be considerate."

"I've convinced Piper to redecorate the villa. She and Zephyr will be in Athens next week and she'll consult with you then on what you want."

"That really *was* thoughtful. Thank you." Though Piper designed the decor for her husband's resorts, she excelled at the type of warm and inviting decor that Polly loved.

"One instance out of how many where I ignored your preferences for expediency or taking my mother's opinions over your own about what *you* needed?"

He really had been listening, but she didn't like her super confident husband in this down spiral. He had made mistakes, but he really was doing his best to rectify them.

"Who was it who took the entire day to shop with me for nursery furniture? Who made sure I rested when I needed to?" And maybe sometimes when she didn't. "Who bought me a second bassinet because I loved it?" She winked. "Who bought that second bassinet even after the very talented furniture maker flirted with me?"

The master carpenter had said Polly had her husband wrapped around her finger. Could it be true? Now?

Were Alexandros's eyes open, and in opening them, had he become genuinely determined to see her as happy as possible?

"You had more in common with him than you do with me."

"Not possible. I have love in common with you, and that's bigger than anything else."

"You think so?"

"I'm beginning to."

His expression turned arrested. "You are."

"Yes."

The kiss they shared was beautiful and hot, and when the car stopped, the only thing Polly wanted to do when they got home was take her husband straight to bed.

Like he was reading her mind, Alexandros slammed the door to their home in the face of the security team.

By the time they reached their bedroom, neither had a stitch of clothing on and Polly's lips were swollen and hot from kissing.

Alexandros lifted her and laid her on the bed as if she was both precious and breakable.

Then he joined her, his expression so intent. "Polly. *Agape mou.*"

They reached for each other at the same time, kissing and touching. The passion between them tinged with love so recently acknowledged.

He was tender.

She was pushy.

When their bodies connected, they both stilled and savored the moment. For the first time in so long, she felt a complete emotional connection with him every bit as deep and real as the physical one.

They moved together, his hands on her body, her hands giving pleasure where she could. She screamed with her orgasm, more tears burnished his eyes with his.

After, he held her close, kissing her temple, whispering words of love in Greek and English.

The walls around Polly's heart crumbled as she accepted that he meant every single utterance. He wasn't perfect, but he was undeniably hers, and she was the one thing he would never willingly give up.

"You never have to see my mother or sister again, if you don't want to," he promised with another soft kiss.

"Is that realistic?" she couldn't help asking.

"They hurt you. They hurt us. We will make it realistic. No one will be allowed to hurt you again on my watch."

"You can't promise that."

"Can't I?"

"Well, your arrogance is back in force, I see." She smiled at her gorgeous husband, thinking more about how happy she was than what they were talking about.

That was probably why it took her a moment to take in the words he was saying.

"We can move to America and be near your family."

"What? What are you saying?"

"I have spoken to Petros, and he can take over running the company. I will take a secondary role in a new American office."

"You? Secondary?" She couldn't imagine.

"I want you happy, and you are not happy here with my family. You will be more content living near yours."

"First, I *am* happy here. Now. Adjusting to life as your wife wasn't easy. I won't pretend otherwise, but I *am* your wife and I love our life in Greece."

"You didn't love it only a few weeks ago."

"I didn't love aspects of it, but we've found compromises to make our family life the stuff of my dreams." They'd even agreed not to have a housekeeper for the penthouse, just some daily cleaning help, so Polly could cook any time she liked and take a more normalized role—for her—in her children's and husband's lives. The villa housekeeper had been very pleased to stay on in the country. "I'm so happy with the way things have been, I'm nearly sick with it."

"I could not tell."

She rested against him, finding a comfortable angle for her pregnant tummy. "I was afraid to show too much, to trust in the changes."

"You thought everything would go back to the way it was."

"Thought? No. Feared? Yes. I'm truly sorry, but yes." She *hadn't* trusted him. Not even a little. No matter how hard he'd been trying, Polly had struggled to believe the changes would be permanent.

But something had changed. Something inside her and maybe something inside him.

"And you do not fear this now?" he asked, like checking the facts.

"No. Now especially, I *know.*" After his offer to give up the legacy his father had left him and move to another country, she really knew. "I know that it's worth fighting for what I need. It's worth fighting for our family."

"But it wasn't before."

"Before, I genuinely believed I wasn't that important to you." That all her fighting and arguing was just wasted energy.

"And now you believe differently?"

"You've made a lot of concessions for my happiness, things I didn't recognize as such even before your rescue bid for our marriage."

"Not enough."

"No, maybe it wasn't enough, not then. At least not for me to keep trusting you with my heart."

"But you trust me now. You told me you love me."

"And I meant it."

"As did I."

"I know."

"You believe." His smile was incandescent.

She was feeling pretty glowy herself. "Yes, I believe."

He took a deep breath, like girding himself to say something difficult. "I think you should consider us moving to America."

"There is no need. I'm not going to think about doing something that will hurt you and I never wanted to begin with."

"But—"

"No, Andros. This is our life and I *can* love this life as long as I know that the children and I are some of your top priorities. That you love me for me, not the emulation of the perfect Greek society wife your mom tried to make me into."

"I have always loved you for you, and I never wanted you to become someone different. Though I can see now that I did a poor job of helping you adjust to our life or believe that. But you and our children are my *top* priorities."

"I'll remind you of that the next time you work until midnight two days in a row."

"Not going to happen."

"It will, sometimes…but that's okay, so long as I know it will be the exception and not the rule."

"A very rare if ever exception."

He was such an overachiever, but she loved that about him, so Polly just smiled. "I bet Petros wasn't keen to take over the company."

"No, he was not, but he agreed."

"What was the stick?"

"What do you mean?"

"A carrot wouldn't have worked. There's no incentive big enough to entice your brother into your role. He's very happy being second in command."

Alexandros shrugged. "If he didn't want to take over, I was going to sell the company."

"What?" Polly sat up and stared down at her too-relaxed husband. "You can't do that. That company is your father's legacy and his father before him."

"Yes, but the legacy I want to build requires you by my side."

"I wasn't going anywhere."

"And now we know you never will, but more importantly, we know that you will be happy staying."

He got so focused when he had a goal. And now she realized she *was* his ultimate goal. "I love you so much, Andros, but sometimes you scare me."

"You have nothing to fear from me."

"No, but I think I'll have to watch out you aren't sacrificing your own happiness for mine going forward."

"I would be honored for you to watch out for my happiness."

Then they were kissing again and whispering more words of love and making promises that lovers make.

EPILOGUE

THEIR SON WAS born a week early and they named him Theodore Robert for his grandfathers.

Polly's mother and father were there and she'd relented at the last minute, calling her mother-in-law when she'd gone into labor and inviting her to the hospital.

Athena had sent Polly a very moving letter of apology beforehand. They'd spoken on the phone a few times, short conversations, but entirely void of the former veiled insults and implications Polly should be doing this, that and the other, differently.

Alexandros had started having lunch with his mother once a week, but never pressured Polly to join him.

His sister hadn't shifted her attitudes at all and therefor had no place in her brother's life. By his choice, not Polly's suggestion.

Maybe one day Stacia would grow up and think of someone else's point of view, but until then, Polly didn't have to deal with the younger woman's poisonous words.

Alexandros never dismissed Polly's opinions now, especially when it came to family life. When they disagreed, they talked. Sometimes, they argued. Heatedly. They were both passionate people. Making up was fun.

And Polly's mom remarked that her daughter was definitely more her headstrong and passionate self than she had been in a long time.

Eight weeks after the birth of their son, Alexandros took Polly on a second honeymoon. They toured the islands on a yacht big enough to accommodate their children, the nursemaids and security. But no one else.

It was a glorious trip, but Polly loved coming home because this time, the honeymoon didn't end with stepping back in Athens.

Her attentive husband continued being loving and wonderful amidst everyday life.

* * * * *

Swept away by
After the Billionaire's Wedding Vows...?
*Enter Lucy Monroe's passionate world
with these other stories!*

An Heiress for His Empire
A Virgin for His Prize
Kostas's Convenient Bride
The Spaniard's Pleasurable Vengeance

Available now!

WE HOPE YOU ENJOYED
THIS BOOK FROM

Escape to exotic locations where passion knows no bounds.

Welcome to the glamorous lives of royals and billionaires, where passion knows no bounds. Be swept into a world of luxury, wealth and exotic locations.

8 NEW BOOKS AVAILABLE EVERY MONTH!

#3893 THE SHEIKH'S MARRIAGE PROCLAMATION
by Annie West

When Tara Michaels arrives on Sheikh Raif's doorstep fleeing a forced betrothal, he knows protecting her will be risky—but entranced by her stubborn beauty, he knows one way to keep her safe... He must make her his bride!

#3894 CROWNING HIS INNOCENT ASSISTANT
The Kings of California
by Millie Adams

Countless women would be thrilled to marry King Matteo de la Cruz. Yet his brilliant personal assistant, Livia, flat out refuses his proposal...and then *quits*! Matteo is outraged, then intrigued... Can anything make his ideal queen reconsider?

#3895 PRIDE & THE ITALIAN'S PROPOSAL
by Kate Hewitt

Fiery Liza is the last woman Fausto should marry. But this proud Italian can't resist the way she challenges him. He's determined to fight fire with fire—by claiming Liza with a shocking proposal!

#3896 TERMS OF THEIR COSTA RICAN TEMPTATION
The Diamond Inheritance
by Pippa Roscoe

Skye Soames's search for her family's long-lost diamonds leads her to Benoit Chalendar's mansion in the Costa Rican rain forest. The billionaire offers to help her find the diamonds—*if* she agrees to a marriage pact to save his company!

"I judge on what I see," Fausto said as he captured her queen easily. She
looked unfazed by the move, as if she'd expected it, although to Fausto's
eye, it had seemed a most inexpert choice. "Doesn't everyone do the
same?"

"Some people are more accepting than others."

"Is that a criticism?"

"You seem cynical," Liza said.

"I consider myself a realist," Fausto returned, and she laughed, a
crystal clear sound that seemed to reverberate through him like the ringing
of a bell.

"Isn't that what every cynic says?"

"And what are you? An optimist?" He imbued the word with the
necessary skepticism.

"I'm a realist. I've learned to be." For a second she looked bleak, and
Fausto realized he was curious.

"And where did you learn that lesson?"

She gave him a pert look, although he still saw a shadow of that
unsettling bleakness in her eyes. "From people such as yourself." She
moved her knight—really, what was she thinking there? "Your move."

Fausto's gaze quickly swept the board and he moved a pawn. "I
don't think you know me well enough to have learned such a lesson," he
remarked.

"I've learned it before, and in any case, I'm a quick study." She looked
up at him with glinting eyes, a coy smile flirting about her mouth. A mouth
Fausto had a sudden, serious urge to kiss. The notion took him so forcefully
and unexpectedly that he leaned forward a little over the game, and Liza's
eyes widened in response, her breath hitching audibly as surprise flashed
across her features.

For a second, no more, the very air between them felt tautened, vibrating with sexual tension and expectation. It would be so very easy to close the space between their mouths. So very easy to taste her sweetness, drink deep from that lovely, luscious well.

Of course, he was going to do no such thing. He could never consider a serious relationship with Liza Benton. She was not at all the sort of person he was expected to marry, and in any case, he'd been burned once before, when he'd been led by something so consuming and changeable as desire.

As for a cheap affair… The idea had its tempting merits, but he knew he had neither the time nor inclination to act on it. An affair would be complicated and distracting, a reminder he needed far too much in this moment.

Fausto leaned back, thankfully breaking the tension, and Liza's smile turned catlike, surprising him. She looked so knowing, as if she'd been party to every thought in his head, which thankfully she hadn't been, and was smugly informing him of that fact.

"Checkmate," she said softly.

Jolted, Fausto stared at her blankly before glancing down at the board. "That's impossible," he declared as his gaze moved over the pieces. And with another jolt, he realized it wasn't. She'd put him in checkmate and he hadn't even realized his king had been under threat. He'd indifferently moved a pawn while she'd neatly spun her web. Disbelief warred with a scorching shame as well as a reluctant admiration. While he'd assumed she'd been playing an amateurish, inexperienced game, she'd been neatly and slyly laying a trap.

"You snookered me."

Her eyes widened with laughing innocence. "I did no such thing. You just assumed I wasn't a worthy opponent." She cocked her head, her gaze turning flirtatious—unless he was imagining that? Feeling it? "But, of course, you judge on what you see."

The tension twanged back again, even more electric than before. Slowly, deliberately, Fausto knocked over his king to declare his defeat. The sound of the marble clattering against the board was loud in the stillness of the room, the only other sound their suddenly laboured breathing.

He had to kiss her. He would. Fausto leaned forward, his gaze turning sleepy and hooded as he fastened it on her lush mouth. Liza's eyes flared again and she drew an unsteady breath, as loud as a shout in the still, silent room. Then, slowly, deliberately, she leaned forward…

Don't miss
Pride & the Italian's Proposal.
Available March 2021 wherever
Harlequin Presents books and ebooks are sold.

Harlequin.com

HPEXP0221

Get 4 FREE REWARDS!

We'll send you 2 FREE Books plus <u>2</u> FREE Mystery Gifts.

Harlequin Presents books feature the glamorous lives of royals and billionaires in a world of exotic locations, where passion knows no bounds.

FREE Value Over $20
